Salems Song
The Curse Of The Blood Moon

Kristen Proby

Ampersand
Publishing, Inc.

Salems Song
A Curse of the Blood Moon Novel
By
Kristen Proby

SALEMS SONG

A Curse of the Blood Moon Novel

Kristen Proby

For Kathy.
I love you more.

PROLOGUE
KATRINA HARWOOD

September 1692

"We must make haste." I have never written so quickly, and I pray to all the gods and goddesses that the special ink I'm using will work how it should.

"There are no words on the page, my love."

I do not spare my sweet husband a look as I keep going.

"I have cast a spell on the ink, Thomas," I reply. "I must finish writing this before he casts the curse."

"Of whom are you speaking?"

I can hear the frustration in his voice, but there is simply no time to explain. I know, down to the marrow of my bones, that Jonas will cast the curse of the blood moon this night, despite all the begging and warning I have done.

My brother believes it is the only way to protect his coven.

"Jonas," I mutter, still writing. "I must get this down."

Line by line, I write the words I have memorized over the past weeks, knowing this may be the only way to break the curse once Jonas casts it.

However, once it is done, no one, not even I, will remember what has transpired.

Tears fall unchecked down my cheeks, and I rush on. I despise the few precious seconds it takes to dip my quill into the special ink so I may continue.

Please, Jonas. Please, do not do it yet.

I do not know if Jonas can hear my plea, but I send it out anyway and continue my quest.

Once I've written the spell, I continue with the instructions. I must get it all down and trust that it will not all be in vain.

"Darling, we must go."

"I know. I just need one more moment."

"Katrina—"

"There. 'Tis done."

I sit back in the chair and blow out a long, relieved breath. More than anything, I wish I could see my dear brother and embrace him, pull him close and reassure us both that everything will be as it should be in the end.

But this must do for now.

"I do not think I forgot anything."

"What will he do, Katrina?"

Finally, I raise my eyes to my beloved and see worry and fear on his handsome face.

"What he believes is right."

"And is it?"

I close my eyes and feel the hot tears running down my cheeks. "My dreams are full of despair, Thomas. The premonitions do not end well."

"Will they die?"

I find his gaze with mine once more. "'Tis a fate worse than death. They will not remember, and they will *never* die."

His brow furrows in confusion, and then he blinks and stares down at my Book of Shadows. "What are you doing there?"

It has begun.

There is but a moment of pain in my heart, but then it's as though I am waking from a long slumber. I look down at my book with a frown. "I must have run out of ink."

But I notice a notation in my handwriting, telling me not to write or mark on the blank pages.

Odd. I don't remember why.

"We must make haste," Thomas says, gathering the last of his things to stow in the wagon. "It is not safe for us here, my love."

Sorrow fills me. I love my home in Salem so much, but I know he is right.

We must go.

"I am ready. This is the last of my things."

"Come, then. We leave tonight."

I nod and follow my love out of our small home on Chestnut Street, then turn to look back inside. With a wave of my hand, all the candles extinguish, and the fire dies. Our cabin is empty.

As much as I do not want to go, it is the only way to ensure our survival.

Chapter One
Lorelei

"We're supposed to be fishing here, Xander."

My comment doesn't deter his hands—or his mouth—from moving over my body in that delicious way he does that never fails to set my heart and every nerve ending in my body on fire. I've known for as long as I can remember that Xander would be my forever. That he would be the one I loved, cherished, and committed myself to for all time.

I believe we've been linked for many lifetimes.

"That's what I wanted you to think," he mumbles against the soft skin of my neck, sending shivers down my arms. "I just wanted to get you alone."

"You have a house."

"On the water," he clarifies, and I look up into those dark, fathomless eyes of his. They're the color of black tourmaline, and I've never felt safer than when I'm looking into his eyes. "I want you on the water, Lorelei."

That's not a surprise. He always wants me on the water. As a sea witch, and with water being my most powerful element, the sex out here is out of this fucking world.

The winds are calm, the bay around us hardly rocking us at all as I reach back to unzip my dress and let it fall away from my arms, pooling at my feet.

Most men would let their eyes roam over a naked woman's body, but not my Xander. No, his black orbs stay on mine as his hands glide down my arms to link with mine.

"You're way overdressed."

"You're the most beautiful woman any of the gods or goddesses have ever created."

And just like that, he knocks the wind right out of me. Xander makes me feel so cherished, so damn alive when we're together. I'm simply addicted to him. I can't get enough.

And I know, without a doubt, that he feels the same way about me.

In our early twenties, we're just starting to find our way in the world, in our coven, and with each other.

But one thing is always a constant.

Each other.

"Will it always be like this?"

He lifts an eyebrow in question, and I swallow hard, not entirely sure why I said that. It just popped into my head and tumbled out.

"Us. This. Will it always be so...big? So fucking all-

encompassing and overwhelming and just...everything important in the world?"

He blinks rapidly, obviously surprised, and then moves in closer, guiding me down to the blanket he spread out on the bottom of the boat.

That should have been my first clue that there would be no fishing tonight.

"Yes," he says at last, his voice firm and strong. "Absolutely. Because I'll never let you go, Lorelei."

"Okay, that sounds a little—"

"Not in a crazy way," he says with a deep chuckle, leaning in to kiss my cheek near my ear. "I'm so in love with you that if you were to ever leave me, it would break me in two."

My exhale of relief is immediate. "I feel the exact same way."

The wind picks up enough to blow through my hair, and Xander brushes it off my face and then kisses me. Softly at first, and then with more intensity and fervor. I feel the boat begin to rock with our passion.

"So fucking beautiful," he murmurs again, letting his hands travel over my skin to my breasts, then over my ribs.

"Why aren't I cold?"

"I put us in a little, warm bubble," he says with a proud smile. Xander is an incredibly powerful witch. He's been shifting into animals since he hit puberty. He can manipulate the elements, read minds, speak to the dead...

He's incredible.

And he's all mine.

"I like this warm bubble." I reach for the buttons on his black shirt and begin unfastening them. "I'll like it more when you're naked and inside me."

That makes him pick up his pace just a little. He shucks out of his clothes, careful to keep them from flying overboard, and then I'm straddling him, rubbing my center on his long, hard, smooth length.

"For the love of Zeus," he hisses between his teeth as he braces my hips in his hands, helping me to move against him. "You're the only thing in the universe that makes me lose myself."

With a smile, I lift up and reach down to position him perfectly so I can sink over him and watch as those black eyes go heavy with pleasure.

It took my body a while to get used to him at the beginning of our relationship. Xander is tall, well over six and a half feet, and he has the cock to go with the height.

He's always been careful with me, but I've adjusted to him now, and absolutely absorbed in the pleasure between us, I ride him.

The wind is wild, the waves churning, and I move on him at a pace that matches the rhythm of the water.

Thunder sounds far away, but we don't break the perfect rhythm of the moment.

"Love you," I mutter over and over again as I chase down the orgasm building inside me. "Goddess, I love you so much, Xander."

"Ah, baby." He tips my chin up with his fingers. "Eyes on me, Siren."

My lids immediately open, and with our eyes locked and his hands on the globes of my ass, we come together, letting all our love spill into each other, right here on the open water.

"*Did you just call me* Siren?" *I ask when I can finally breathe again and pull my dress back on.*

"*I did.*"

He grins at me as he buttons his shirt, and I can't help but think it's such a shame for him to cover that gorgeous body.

"*You tempt me like a siren. And you're just as beautiful.*"

"*And dangerous.*" *I narrow my eyes at him, but he doesn't lose his smile at all. "I'm serious. I'm a dangerous woman.*"

"*Oh, I'm aware.*"

"*But I don't scare you.*"

More thunder and lightning rage around us, catching our attention. This isn't our doing.

"*We'd better get to shore," I say. Suddenly, the boat rocks violently as if something is beneath it, trying to tip it over. "Oh, shit, Xander.*"

"*Hold on," he says, passing me a rope. "Do* not *let go of this. Do you hear me?*"

"*This is bad.*" *I shake my head, watching the water around us. I decide to cast a spell to calm it down. "Gods of my element, goddesses of seas, lend me your power to put the water at ease. Calm the storm and temper the tide, smooth out the waves on which we ride. Protect us herein and those on the land; settle yourself before this gets out of hand."*

That should have worked, but it does nothing.

"Xander, what is this?"

"Lorelei."

My head whips around at the horrific sound of his voice, and I scream when I see that he's torn to shreds. His skin hangs loosely off his bones, and I try to get over to him. Before I can, the boat capsizes and tosses me into the water.

"Lorelei."

I gasp and sit up, thrashing as if I'm still under that horrible water, but then I'm suddenly in Xander's strong arms, and he's rocking me, holding me close.

"Shh," he coos. "You're okay. It's okay, Lorelei."

He hasn't called me by any term of endearment in years.

Because I forbade him to do it.

Because of what happened.

"Why are you here?"

The briefest look of hurt crosses his face. I would have missed it if I didn't know him as intimately as I do.

But I *do* know him.

My body still hums from that fucked-up dream. And the worst part is, I've been having similar ones almost every night. Memories of our time together, back when things were so good that I thought nothing could ever tear us apart. And then, the end of the dream is so messed up I stay awake the rest of the night, trying to calm down from it.

"You were screaming," he says flatly, standing from the porch swing where I'd curled up for a nap.

Napping is another thing I've been doing. Thanks to horny and messed-up nightmares at night.

"Really?" I wipe my eyes and frown. "Weird."

If he's going to be so close to me, my body *really* needs to calm the hell down. Because Xander is the one person in this universe that I *can't* have.

Not ever again.

"It was only a nightmare."

His eyes, those beautiful black eyes, narrow on my face as if searching for answers that I'm not willing to give him. "What kind of nightmare?"

"Just a stupid one. Tomorrow is October. Breena and Giles just got married less than a week ago, and Samhain is just around the corner. That means we've got some stress going on here, you know?"

I shrug like it's no big deal, but he and I both know it *is* a big deal.

We're trying to lift a curse that's been in place for three centuries.

"Xander, I have a question."

"Anything."

I lick my lips and stand, wrapping my arms around my middle as I walk closer to the water that laps against the shore barely twenty yards away from my little cottage.

"Do you think we really got rid of the...*thing* that tried to kill us over Beltane?"

I turn to find him frowning at me. Goddess, he's a

beautiful man. In every way. And my body, my heart, it all yearns for him every time I look at him.

It's a form of torture that I wouldn't wish on anyone. Because I can't have him. After what happened before, there's no possibility of us being together.

"No, I don't." His statement brings me back to the here and now.

"Why didn't you say something at the time?"

"Because we all needed to believe we had. We needed the respite, and it wasn't a danger to us then."

I worry my bottom lip and shift my feet.

"It's not gone. I know it's not."

"Is that what the nightmare was about?"

"Maybe," I whisper and look back out at the water. I take a deep breath and then look at him once more. "You said I was screaming, but how did you know that?"

"I was flying overhead." He says it so matter-of-factly I have to blink twice.

"Why were you flying over my house?"

"To check on you, of course."

"Xander, I don't need you to check on me."

"Too fucking bad." His voice is still calm, his face impassive. "I can fly wherever I godsdamn well please, and if that means I want to look in on you to make sure you're safe, then I fucking will, Lorelei. You don't have a say in that."

"You're so damn irritating."

"Back at you."

He makes me want to pull my hair out at the roots,

but I also want to run over there and hug him in gratitude. Because as much as I insist that I don't need him, it does soothe me knowing that Xander's looking out for me.

He's the most powerful witch and the strongest *man* I know.

"Also, we can ride together over to Jonas and Lucy's place for dinner," he adds.

"Are you going to give me a ride on your back?"

"I was thinking we could go in your car like normal people."

I can't help but bust out laughing at that, and I see the humor in his eyes, as well. "There is absolutely *nothing* normal about you and me, Xander."

"Maybe not, but we can pretend. Come on, give a weary traveler a ride."

It'll mean being close to him, and with the dream still fresh in my mind, I want to say, "*Absolutely not.*"

But I've also been making a concentrated effort to be a little nicer to Xander since everything went down on Beltane.

If we don't work together, we will fail.

And that's not an option for us.

"Yeah, okay. Let me grab my purse, and you can hitch a ride with me."

"**M**arriage looks good on you." I lean in and hug my sweet cousin, Breena, and then offer her new husband, Giles, a kiss on the cheek. There's a *lot* of sexual energy humming around them. Their auras are even bright red. "Have you had a good honeymoon?"

"The best." Breena beams. "It was so nice to take the week to be together, but now it's time to get back down to business. Tomorrow is the start of October, meaning we only have one month to get our act together."

"I think our act is pretty well together," Lucy, my other cousin, says as she sets a pan of bread on the table. She grins at her husband, Jonas, as he rubs his hand in a big circle over her back.

I can't believe both of my cousins, who are as close to me as sisters, got married in less than a year.

It's mind-boggling, actually.

Especially considering that Jonas was born in the middle of the seventeenth century and lives in an invisible village stuck in the year 1692.

But I guess what they say is true: *If it's meant to be, it'll find a way.*

Or something like that.

"You're pretty quiet," Giles says to me with a kind smile. "What's up?"

"Oh, nothing. I napped this afternoon, and you know how you take a nap, and then when you wake up, you're not sure what year it is, let alone the day or time?"

"I hate when that happens," Breena says.

"Yeah, well, I guess I'm still clearing away the cobwebs. Lucy, what can I do to help?"

"Everything is done," she says, gesturing for us all to sit at her gorgeous table. "I know we need to get to work, but I thought it would be nice if we had a good meal first."

"I'm not complaining," Xander says and loads up his plate. The man has always had a bottomless stomach. He will eat anything and everything in sight. And then have dessert.

Twice.

Once upon a time, the dessert was *me*.

Oh, for fuck's sake. Stop it.

"How's the tapestry coming along, Breena?"

Grateful for Xander's question and something else for me to think about, I look over at my cousin and feel something resembling concern settle in my stomach.

"It's going, but part of it got wet last night. I'm worried that the colors will run." She shakes her head mournfully. "I might have to unravel that piece and redo it. Which I can totally do. It just means more time."

"How did it get wet?" I ask her.

"That's the kicker," Giles jumps in. "We don't know. There wasn't a leak in the ceiling, and nothing spilled."

It's him.

The voice is as clear as anyone else's in my ear, and I glance around to see who's here with us. Lucy's mom,

Agatha, is always near, but it wasn't her voice that I heard.

I don't see anyone else, so I turn my attention back to those around the table.

"What do you need from us?" I ask. "Will we have to find more wool?"

"Maybe. I'll get some, just to be on the safe side."

"Lorelei and I can dye it," Lucy offers.

"Absolutely," I agree. "And I've collected some more embellishments and put some spells on them for you to add, as well."

"Thanks," Breena says with a smile. "Between all of us, we'll get this figured out. I know Samhain is just a month away, but I have a really good feeling about this."

I watch Jonas sit back in his chair and smile at Breena in that sweet way he does. I know he's completely in love with Lucy and totally dedicated to her, but he has such a soft spot for Breena. It's really sweet when they're together. Almost as if they're siblings or something.

"I will admit," Breena continues, "the scene on the tapestry is different than I expected."

"How so?" Xander asks.

"Well, I went into Hallows End with Jonas so I could see it for myself and weave the scene onto the tapestry. But the image that's showing up is completely foreign to me. It could be that when it's all finished, with all the embellishments and everything, it'll come into focus for me. But I've just been letting my instincts take over."

"That's the best way to do it," Lucy says. "You're a

gifted witch, Breena. Your guides and ancestors won't steer you wrong."

"I hope you're right." Breena's voice has a tiny edge to it, and Giles rubs her back soothingly. "I'm so excited for all this to be finished so we can just get back to our regular lives, you know?"

"I don't know what that will look like," Jonas says, speaking up. "Well, that's not true. It will be a beautiful life with Lucy, of course. But for those in Hallows End? I just don't know."

"We'll roll with it as it happens," I remind him. "That's all any of us can do. We'll be prepared to help everyone."

"And I'm grateful."

"I have a question." Xander swallows his bite of food, his eyes pinned to the back door leading out to Lucy's gardens. "Should we have a conversation about the dead woman in the backyard?"

Chapter Two
Xander

Silence falls over the room as all six pairs of eyes turn to the open back door leading to the gardens beyond.

"I don't see her," Lucy says, frustration hanging heavily in her voice. "Not that that's anything new. I never see any dead people, and I'm damn jealous of that."

"I see her," Lorelei murmurs next to me, and I'm stunned when she instinctively reaches out for my hand, gripping it tightly.

Aside from when everything went down on Beltane, Lorelei hasn't held my hand in *years*.

"What does she look like?" Giles asks.

"She's young," Lorelei answers him. "I'd say...late teens. She has curly blonde hair and is wearing a blue dress."

"It's creepy how she's just watching us," Breena whispers, and Lorelei's gaze whips around to her cousin in surprise.

"You can see her? You've never been a medium before."

"Well, I can see *her*," Breena confirms. "What about you, Jonas?"

"I see." Jonas's voice is hushed, and I turn to study the man with narrowed eyes. I've come to know him well over the past year. Also, he's my many-times-great-uncle. I'm a direct descendant of his sister, Katrina. I've often wondered if that's why I feel such a strong bond with the other man.

"What do you think?" I ask Jonas.

"I remember her." Jonas takes a deep breath, and we all watch as the woman shakes her head, then turns and walks into the woods behind Lucy's home. "Her name was Mildred Hale. She married John Hale about a month before she died in the early seventeen hundreds."

"How do you know, if you were trapped in Hallows End?" Breena asks him.

"Because I had discovered that I could move between worlds by then, and I remember the incident well because it was believed that John murdered his young wife in a psychotic episode. She was brutally tortured before succumbing to her injuries."

"What happened to John?" I ask, but I have a feeling I already know the answer.

"They hanged him the next morning," Jonas replies, confirming my thoughts. "He claimed he was innocent but was found with her, and they immediately carried out the sentence."

"I want to call my mom," Breena says, reaching for her phone. "She and Aunt Astrid know who all the yearly victims were, going back hundreds of years. I wonder if Mildred is on the list."

"She is," Lorelei confirms, looking at the kitchen doorway. "Aunt Agatha just said so."

"Thanks, Mom," Lucy says, sarcasm dripping from every syllable. "You could have told *me*, but no, you won't let me see you."

"She just smirked at you," Lorelei informs Lucy. "Agatha, was Mildred the first victim?"

"What did she say?" Giles asks, leaning forward.

"Yes. She believes so."

"I'll double-check with Mom," Breena adds, typing out a text on her phone.

"I don't know why she would show up *now*," Giles says. "Why wouldn't she have shown herself every year for the past couple of centuries? Have you ever had a ghost in your backyard before, Lucy?"

"Nope."

"I know why." I squeeze Lorelei's hand before standing and walking to the door, shoving my hands into my pockets as I stare out to where the woman was, still seeing her clearly in my mind. "She's warning us."

"We got rid of the son of a bitch." Giles's voice is hard and angry.

"Did we?" Now *Lorelei's* voice is hard with her anger,

and I turn to see the scowl on her gorgeous face—the face that lives in my dreams and haunts my every waking moment.

The woman I'll never get over, no matter how many lifetimes I live, because she's a part of me.

"We saw it happen," Lucy insists, but Lorelei is already shaking her head.

"We defeated it in battle, but that doesn't mean it's *gone.*"

"Well, shit. Then we still have that asshole to deal with on top of breaking the curse?" Giles pushes his hands through his hair with a gusty sigh of disgust. "I'm getting really sick of this piece of shit."

"We don't know for sure he isn't gone," Breena says, ever the optimist. Breena is our peacekeeper, the tenderest of hearts. But even she deflates a little as she looks around the room at all our expressions. "Well, darn."

"What if it wasn't Mildred?" Lucy asks, her voice suddenly shaking. "What if it was *it*, in Mildred's form?"

"Nothing would surprise me." I rub my hand over my face, angry at myself for scaring the others, but they need to know. The more informed everyone is, the more they can protect themselves.

"Back on high alert," Lorelei says, pushing her dark auburn hair off her shoulder. "Awesome. Listen, we shouldn't let this interfere with the task at hand. The curse is our priority. I'm done giving this asshole more attention than he deserves. I'm over letting it bully us."

"Agreed," Jonas says. "And I'm not just saying that out of selfishness because of the curse. I think it feeds off the energy of the fear and anger everyone gives it. So, while we should always remain watchful and guarded, we shouldn't panic."

"Excellent advice," I agree. "I do, however, think it's smart for us to stay in packs. I'll alert the rest of the coven. While we might not intend to give it attention, there's no need to be careless."

Everyone nods in agreement, and I sit at the table once more.

"You're not moving in with me," Lorelei informs me, jutting out her stubborn chin, practically daring me to argue with her.

"I can sit on the front porch. The elements don't bother me."

"You will *not* invade my space."

"Uh-oh, here we go," Breena says with a sigh. "Lorelei, you can't be there by yourself."

"Fuck that," Lorelei shoots back. "I've been on my own for a long time, and I'll be just fine. I'm more powerful than I've ever been. I'm protected."

"We're safer together," Jonas argues. "If you won't let Xander stay with you, come here, or go to Breena and Giles's home."

"Right. Because I want to hang out with all the newlyweds. Look, I'm happy for all of you. Over the moon, in fact. But you're all newly married and need your privacy. I'm *fine*. Why won't you all believe that?"

"You're strong," I agree. Now it's my turn to reach for *her* hand, which I can tell irritates her.

At one time, she longed for my touch. Now, it only makes her angry.

"You're powerful, and you're a force to be reckoned with. All of that is true, Lorelei. But for fuck's sake, use your brain. You know as well as anyone that it's safer when you're not alone."

"Then I'll be taking a risk because you will *not*, under any fucking circumstances, come to live with me. I'm sorry if that hurts your feelings." There's a war raging in her gorgeous green eyes. I can see it. "I really, truly am. But you will never know how having you so close hurts me, and the thought of you being in my space all the time is absolutely unfathomable."

Breena sniffs and wipes a tear from her eye. "I wish I knew what hurt you so badly. Both of you."

But Lorelei will never willingly tell them.

Because even in her anger and pain, she will continue to protect me, even if it's just that much.

At the end of the day, she still loves me.

"I understand," I say at last. "The coven will come and set extra protection wards around your home. You'll use your element and your magick to protect yourself at all times. I mean it, Lora."

"I will," she says with a nod. "Don't worry. It's fine."

"It's fine," Lucy echoes and then chuckles humorlessly. "Right. It's all just *fine*."

L orelei can so easily cut me with words. The fact that it *hurts* her for me to be near her pretty much brings me to my knees.

My instinct is to protect her. From the thing fucking with us, from the dangers of lifting the curse, and from anything else that could possibly harm her. And to do that, I need to be close by, even if it means lurking around the borders of her property as a wolf or a raven and keeping an eye out.

She may not want me with her all the time, but I'll stick close.

I just have to make one last trip out past the bay to the ocean to collect the nets and traps I have out there, and then I'll be on land until after Samhain.

Unfortunately, Lorelei will have to suck it up and go out with me.

I sigh as I climb her front porch steps and rub my hand down my face in agitation before raising my fist to knock on the door.

A few seconds later, she answers, her eyes wide as she looks up at me.

Goddess, she's gorgeous. Every time I see her, it's like a punch to the gut.

"Hey," she says, leaning her shoulder on the doorjamb though not inviting me inside. "What's up?"

"I need a favor."

Her beautiful eyes narrow with suspicion.

"Okay. What's the favor?"

"I need you to ride out with me on the boat to gather my fishing nets and traps."

"Right. Have a nice day."

She moves to shut the door in my face, but I plant my palm on the wood, stopping her.

"No, really."

"I don't know if you're drunk, sick, or what, but I'm not a fisherwoman, Xander. I'm a writer. And I'm behind on my deadline. You pulled me out of my groove."

"Please." She pauses at the sound of my voice. "My crew is all off on other jobs since I decided not to work until after Samhain. I need an extra set of hands and a spotter. Just for a couple of hours. You know the work, Lorelei."

"It's been a really long time."

"I know. And I know you don't like being near me, but I promise to keep my hands to myself, and we will get the job done as fast as possible while still staying safe."

She worries that plump lower lip for a second and then rolls her eyes, letting out a sigh.

"Fine. I'll go change real quick. Give me ten."

She closes the door and leaves me out on the porch, which is fine with me. I see her agreement as a *huge* win.

Could I do it alone? Absolutely. But it's not the safest thing to do, and that would mean leaving the stubborn woman unprotected, and I'm not willing to do that.

Ten minutes turns into fifteen, but Lorelei finally

steps out of the house in thick working pants and a green T-shirt under a heavy plaid shirt. Her hair is pulled back in a ponytail, and she tugs a hat over her head and ears.

"You remember how cold it is on the water."

"It's miserable," she grumbles as she steps around me, already pulling on her gloves. Her brow is furrowed in a scowl, and I want to kiss her there but shove my hands into my pockets instead. "But I remember what to do. Let's get this show on the road so I can get back home."

Happy to take my win, I walk beside Lorelei to her car. She drives us to the marina and my boat slip.

Less than thirty minutes later, we're gliding across the water under clear blue skies, out to where my nets are cast, and my traps are anchored.

I glance over and see the love of my life with her head tilted back and her eyes closed. She's soaking in the breeze coming off the ocean. If you looked up the term *sea witch* in the dictionary, there would probably be a photo of Lorelei.

The autumn sun shines on her face as we glide over the water, a handful of miles from shore.

"There are the first nets," I call out, pointing ahead. Lorelei opens her eyes and nods, ready to help.

I pull in the lines for the next hour, making our way back toward land, and Lorelei helps me guide the nets over the deck to drop the fish we've caught.

My vessel is very small compared to most commercial fishing operations, but it gets the job done.

"Last one," I call out as I pull up a trap and dump some lobsters onto the deck.

"Thank the goddess," Lorelei replies, wiping the back of her sleeve over her forehead. "I'm going to have to take an hour-long shower to get rid of the fish smell."

"Nah, just a regular shower will do it." I grin at her. When she smiles back, it sucks the breath right out of me.

Once, long ago, I used to bring her out onto the water to make love to her. The magic we made together while pulling in the elements around us was always incredibly intense, and it became something I craved often.

She never complained. I think she loved it as much as I did.

Even as psychic as I am, I could never read Lorelei, and she could never read me. We *knew* each other, inside and out, but there was never a psychic link between us, and I often thought that was a good thing. I enjoyed the mystery with her because it was unlike anything I'd ever experienced with anyone else.

Now, I wish more than anything I could read her mind.

"Okay, what's next?" she asks, pulling me out of my thoughts.

"We measure the fish and lobsters that look too small and throw back any that aren't legal, then get everything we're keeping into cold storage below. Then, we'll head back. Shouldn't be long. Thank you for the help. I mean it."

"I always enjoy being out on the water," she says with a shrug. But despite not being able to read her mind, I can see that something is bothering her.

"What's wrong?"

She shakes her head, but I walk to her and take her shoulders in my hands.

"What's wrong, Lorelei?"

"I've had a bad feeling all day," she admits, her voice low as she glances around nervously. "Maybe it's because of what happened at Lucy's yesterday, and my mind is just playing tricks on me."

"Your gut never lies," I reply simply, watching her closely. "I'll get you home."

"Xander." She swallows hard, peering up at me. I notice that the wind has picked up a bit, but that's not unusual this far out into the ocean. "I don't like being afraid all the time."

"I know, baby."

Without any prompting, Lorelei leans into me, wraps her arms around me, and rests her cheek on my chest, clinging to me.

"I know I shouldn't do this. It's stupid and unfair to us both," she admits. "But damn it, this is our *place*. And I just need a minute."

"You can have all the minutes you want." My body hums in awareness. Not just sexual, though that's always under the surface with Lorelei. It's the knowledge that I can touch her, be so close to her, that has my entire being on high alert.

"It's not fair," she says again, shaking her head. "It sends you mixed messages, and it's not fair."

"It *is* mixed messages," I agree and then laugh when she glares up at me. "Hey, you said it first."

"You're supposed to say it's okay."

"Nothing about us is okay, and you know it."

She rests her cheek on my chest once more without answering me, and we stay like that for a long moment, pulling in the power of the water and the air around us. I always felt so fucking strong after being out here with her, and this is no different.

Not only is it *our* special place, but it also bolsters our powers, and that always led to amazing sex.

Not that the sex wasn't *always* out of this fucking universe. It was just different on the water.

But that's not what we're here for.

"We have to go back," I murmur, but she only holds on more tightly. "Lorelei, talk to me."

"Something is about to happen."

"Where?"

"Right here. Shit, Xander. I dreamed this, and if it happens like it did in my dream, then you're going to die. And I swear to all the gods and goddesses, if you die on me, I will never forgive you."

"Whoa. I'm not going to die today, and neither are you. What's going to happen?"

She looks up at me, and I see her eyes are black. She opens her mouth, but no words come out.

"Shit."

I take her shoulders in my hands once more and begin chanting a spell.

"I call on the Water and the Air in surplus, banish that which tries to destroy us. I call on the Earth of the ocean and the Fire of the sun, protect us and guide us, thy will be done."

There's a scream on the wind, and then Lorelei blinks. I see her eyes clear, going back to their deep, moss green.

"What in the actual hell?"

"I'm getting you home," I reply as clouds form above and lightning streaks across the sky. "If you could work a calming spell for this water, that would help a lot."

"On it," she says, her arms already moving as she begins her spell. It works. The wind dies down, and the clouds clear. Within minutes, I can see the shoreline.

Lorelei doesn't stop speaking the spell, chanting it over and over again until I've docked the boat, taken her hand, and led her ashore.

We turn together to look out at the harbor and bay, seeing that the ocean beyond is perfectly calm, the sun shining, and birds flying as if nothing at all happened.

"Please, Lorelei, let me stay with you."

"No." It's a whisper, with less heat behind it than she had yesterday. "I can't, Xander."

"And I can't leave you alone. So, what do you propose we do?"

"I don't know." She shakes her head slowly. "I guess I could move in with my mom and aunt. Technically, I can work from anywhere."

"You need the water. They don't live on the water."

She lifts her gaze to mine, and I see her lower lip tremble. Then, she firms it and squares her shoulders. It's as if she reminded herself to be fierce.

"I'm sorry. I know I'm only giving you more mixed messages, but you *can't* stay in my house, Xander. You just can't."

"Lora—"

Before I can argue further, both of our phones ring.

"Damn it."

CHAPTER THREE
LORELEI

Saved by the damn bell.

"Hello?" With my phone at my ear, I silently will my heart to stop hammering in my chest. I was *this close* to conceding and allowing Xander to stay with me.

And as Julia Roberts once said, "*Big mistake. Huge.*"

"Are you okay?" Breena demands in my ear.

"I'm fine. Are *you* okay?" Xander walks a few steps away, his phone also pressed to his ear, talking intently to whoever is on the other end of the line.

"I'm mad," Breena replies. "*Really* mad. And headed right into pissed off."

"What happened?" The scene from the boat only moments ago pops into my mind. "Were you attacked?"

"I was toyed with," she says, indignation heavy in her voice.

Xander ends his phone call and returns to my side. "That was Jonas. He and Lucy just had an...experience."

"So did Breena," I reply. "Breen, where are you?"

"I'm at Giles's shop. Did Xander just say that Jonas and Lucy had something happen, too?"

"Yeah. Are you two able to meet us at Lucy's?"

"We're on our way."

Breena hangs up, and Xander immediately takes my elbow, leading me to my car.

"Sounds like the bastard had fun with all six of us at once," he says, his handsome-as-sin face drawn into lines of worry as he types out a text on his phone. Probably getting someone to come and take care of the catch on the boat. It'd be a shame to let it go to waste.

"There was no real power behind what happened out there," I remind him as he finishes and puts down his phone. "It was just an attempt to frighten us."

"He fucked with us in our place." He wipes his hand over his mouth as I drive across town to Lucy's. "And that on its own means that I'll destroy him. Once and for all. He'll pay for all of it."

Whenever Xander is in this mood, I know not to antagonize him. Not because I'm afraid of him, but because he's in what I always called *intense witch mode*. And while it's incredibly interesting to watch, I've also always found it sexy as hell.

He's just so big and broody and absolutely a force to be reckoned with.

I see Giles and Breena parking just as we reach Lucy's. All four of us go into the apothecary together.

Nothing looks amiss in the Blood Moon Apothecary, but I can feel the energy, and it makes my hackles rise.

"Oh, I don't like this."

Xander says nothing, but the look on his face is grim.

"I couldn't leave Merlin at the shop," Breena says, holding her black cat familiar in her arms. When Nera, the Irish Wolfhound who happens to be Lucy's familiar, runs over to greet Merlin, Breena sets the cat on the floor, and the two animals rub against each other, then curl up together on a bed in the corner.

"I love that they're friends," Lucy says with a grin as she gestures for us to follow her through the doorway to the kitchen, waving at her assistant, Delia. "I'll be back here if you need anything."

"I've got this," Delia says with a wink. "Take your time."

"She's a gem," I announce as I sit in a chair and accept a cup of tea from Jonas. I take a sniff and confirm my suspicion that it contains a protection tincture.

Jonas is always looking out for us like that.

"I don't know what I would do without her," Lucy agrees. "Okay, I'm just going to run down what happened here really quick."

"It happened so fast," Jonas adds.

"Superfast," Lucy agrees. "But there's no doubt that it was *it*. The doors blew open, and the wind picked up like crazy. There was a loud scream, like the one it made both times we defeated it, as if it was hurt and angry."

"It's likely both," Xander says, his voice as cool as a cucumber.

"And then it made a *tornado* in the center of the shop," Lucy continues. "When I looked at Jonas, his eyes were black."

"Same thing happened at Gems," Giles says. "But it was Breena's eyes that turned black."

"We were on Xander's boat," I add. "There was a ton of wind. Xander's eyes are always black, so I can't help there."

"But Lorelei's eyes were black."

My head whips around to stare at Xander. "*What*?"

"Black as night. Creepy as shit."

"So creepy," Giles agrees.

"Your shop looks perfect," I say to Lucy. "If there was a tornado in here, why wasn't it destroyed?"

"That's just it. *Nothing* was moved," Lucy says. "The wind just stopped, and everything was totally normal afterward—as if nothing at all had happened."

"Same at Gems," Breena adds.

"I noticed the same when we got to shore. It was as if nothing happened."

"So, it can scare us, but that's about it right now," Xander says. "That's good news."

"The bad news is that it's gaining strength," Jonas replies. "Stay on alert."

"My wards are about to be so strong and powerful

with a mirror spell that will shoot everything it gives right back to it and punch it in the fucking face," I decide, still fuming. "This fucker won't know what hit him."

"I like that enthusiasm," Jonas says with a grin. "I think we'll all follow suit."

"How's the tapestry?" I ask Breena. "Did you have to re-weave that part of it?"

"Only a little," Breena replies. "And I already got the new wool, dyed it, and spun it. I'm ready to get started again."

"I thought Lucy and I were going to dye it for you."

"I had everything on hand, and it wasn't much," Breena assures me. "It didn't take long. In fact, I should get home and start weaving again. I just went to the shop to have lunch with my new husband when all hell broke loose."

"I'm glad we all reached out to each other," Xander says. "There's power in knowledge."

"We'll do the same again if anything else happens," Jonas says.

"I'll see you guys tomorrow," I say to Breena and Lucy. "For the Samhain celebration committee meeting."

"Why did we agree to do this when we already have such full plates?" Lucy wonders as we all walk through the apothecary to the front door.

"Because we wanted a sense of normalcy," Breena reminds her. "It might have been a bad idea."

"It'll be fun. We're just on décor duty for the lampposts in town. Nothing crazy."

"See you tomorrow," Lucy says. "Stay safe."

"You, too."

I move to get into my car and frown when Xander walks around to the passenger side.

"Where do you think you're going?"

"With you."

He folds his tall form into the seat, and I scowl at him after taking mine.

"You usually just fly away."

"I'm sticking close to you."

I growl as I start my car and pull away from Lucy's, headed toward my cottage on the shore.

"I told you. You're not staying with me."

"I'm still sticking close by."

"You have your own house. Hell, you even have your own car, although I bet it has less than five thousand miles on it, given that you just fly everywhere."

"It's maintaining its value." Xander shrugs, and I decide to ignore him entirely until I get home.

Which doesn't take long.

Pushing out of my car, I let the door slam behind me and stroll up the porch steps to my door without looking back.

But then I hear a *meow* and turn to see a black cat pacing in front of the car.

"You're not going to sucker me into it."

I turn, unlock my door, close it behind me, and get to work.

Walking along the shoreline is my favorite way to start every single day. Even before I've had coffee, I throw on one of my red cloaks and head out with a basket in hand—of course—and stroll along the sand and rock beach. I find things the ocean has left for me. Shells, stones, driftwood.

Today is no different.

I've collected some sea glass and several gorgeous shells that will look fabulous in the new terrarium I'm building. I sit on the log that's been out here for as long as I can remember—my mother lived here before I did—and take a long, deep breath to begin my meditation.

For thirty minutes, I breathe and let my mind wander. I have a garden in my mind, one that sits next to the seaside, of course, where I tend to flowers, chat with birds and squirrels, and just let myself *be*.

I have thoughts of my cousins, and, of course, Xander. He is never far from my mind, despite how much I hate it. But today, it's not thoughts of disdain or betrayal that rise, but rather humor.

I don't like that I'm beginning to soften so much where he's concerned. I should still hate him with every fiber of my being. I should want him to suffer. I shouldn't trust him.

Yet Xander's always been the one person in the world I trust above anyone else, even my mother, aunts, and cousins. And despite everything that went down, that hasn't changed.

I would trust him with my life.

And so, during this meditation, I see Xander walking toward me. With a smile, he takes my hand and begins dancing with me on the shoreline the way we used to do. *Before*.

It made me feel safe, loved, and cherished.

Right now, I need to conjure that feeling. I wouldn't ever ask it of him now, so here, in the safety of my mind, I bring it to the forefront and enjoy some easy time with the man I've always craved.

Finally, though, it's time to let go. I take one last deep breath and say goodbye to Xander in my mind.

His dark eyes are sad as he walks away.

I open my eyes and look out at the sea. It's stormy this morning, the water gray with white-tipped waves churning. It seems to match my mood.

Suddenly, I hear music.

It's faint at first, as if coming from far away, so I narrow my eyes and cock my head, listening more carefully. I don't recognize the tune, but it's absolutely beautiful, and I want to hear more, need to hear it more clearly.

I stand and walk toward the water, so drawn to the music as it grows in volume and strength. It's just so beautiful.

Suddenly, I feel fur beneath my fingers and glance down to see a black wolf staring up at me.

"Hey." I blink rapidly, glancing around. The music is gone. My fingers absently stroke the animal's thick, soft fur. "Did you hear that music? It was so pretty, but I don't hear it now."

I swallow hard, suddenly a little nauseated.

"Someone must have been playing over on the pier or something, and the wind carried it over here."

I glance down at Xander. Although the wolf is *big*, I don't have to bend over to pet him.

"Ugh, I wonder if I ate something bad last night." I start to walk along the shore, headed toward home. "I had some leftover chicken that I heated up, and it seemed fine, but I'm a little queasy this morning. I'd better throw out the rest."

The wolf doesn't reply in any way as he walks beside me. Xander's been close by since we returned from Lucy's house yesterday. He was the cat for a while. Once, I saw the raven flying overhead through my office window.

And now, this morning, he's the wolf.

"You know, I've often wondered why I've never had a familiar." I pat his back companionably as we walk closer to the cottage. "And then it occurred to me, I don't need one. I have you."

That has him stopping and staring up at me as he tilts his head to the side as if asking, "*What the fuck?*"

I laugh and shake my head. "It's true. You're all the animals I can stand. What about you? Have you ever had a familiar? You've never mentioned one."

I'm walking away as I ask, so when Xander replies, it startles me.

"No, I've never had a familiar."

I look back in surprise and see him standing behind me, so tall, broad, and imposing.

And so fucking *gorgeous.*

Why does he have to look like that?

"Did you go home to sleep at all?"

"No."

"Xander. This is just silly. You need to sleep and eat and keep yourself strong."

"I caught a couple of hours on the roof of your cottage, and I've had plenty to eat."

"Don't make me feel guilty."

I stop and turn to him once more, planting my hand on his chest. I feel something surge, moving through my palm, up my arm, and to my heart.

The energy that sparks between us almost brings me to my knees.

"I'm not doing that."

I lick my lips. "But you *are.*"

"I'm an adult, Lorelei. If you don't want me to stay with you to protect you, I respect that. But that doesn't mean I won't stay close."

"If you stayed in human form rather than becoming a bird, a wolf, or a cat, I could have you arrested for stalking."

His lips tip up in an amused grin. "Good thing I can shift, then, isn't it?"

"Stalker status doesn't become you."

"You know that's not what I'm doing." He removes my hand from his chest and holds on to it. "If we didn't have some psychopath supernatural asshole trying to kill us, I'd leave you be—the way I've done for years, Lora. I'm not stalking, I'm fucking *protecting* you."

"I know." My response surprises us both, as evidenced by how he steps back from me. "I know you are, and I'm actually grateful. And annoyed. I'm both."

"I guess I can live with that."

I pull my hand from his and feel the absence instantly.

"I have a meeting with the ladies in an hour, and I haven't had coffee or breakfast." I step up onto the porch and then sigh gustily. I also immediately feel better. The nausea is gone. "Come on in. I'll share with you."

"I won't turn down some coffee."

I walk back to the kitchen and put on a pot of coffee to brew, then scramble up some eggs and toss in some vegetables and bacon.

Xander pours himself a mug of coffee, then does the same for me. He knows the way I like it.

I thank him when he hands me the mug with the spoon still stirring on its own.

"How was Salem last night?"

"Calm." He sips and leans his hip on my countertop, watching me cook. "Everything was chill, which was a relief."

"I placed all new wards, cleansed my crystals before

putting them back in the four corners of the cottage, and set some pretty serious mirror spells. Oh, and I cast a cord-cutting spell."

"I know."

My eyes fly to his. "You watched?"

"I never could resist watching you work your Craft, Lorelei. It's...sexy as fuck."

I bark out a laugh at his honesty and plate his eggs, passing them to him.

"At least, you're honest."

"Pretty much always." He takes a bite. "Mm, these are good. You always hated to cook."

"I learned in California. Took some classes." I frown at my plate as I remember the two years I spent on the West Coast, teaching folklore at a university there. I ran as far from Salem as I could to lick my wounds and heal.

I didn't think I'd ever come back.

"I also learned how to knit, work with watercolors, and do general auto mechanics."

That has his eyebrows climbing into his hairline. "Which are you best at?"

"Auto mechanics, for sure."

He grins at me in that way he always did that tells me he thinks I'm adorable, and I decide I'd better get ready for my meeting.

"I have to get dressed. You don't need to run off. Finish your breakfast. I'll be out in a few."

I hurry back to my bedroom and take a deep breath.

Goddess, why do I have to love him so much? Why can't I just fucking *hate* him?

———

"**B**lack cats are so...*cliché*," Marydell Roberts says with a frown. "I mean, sure, they have their place, but it's expected. Salem, Halloween, witches, and black cats."

"What would you suggest we use instead?" Cindy Sanderson, who is absolutely *not* a friend of ours, frowns at Marydell. "A raccoon? A sloth?"

"There's no need to get snide," Marydell tells Cindy, looking down her nose at the other woman.

Marydell has been on Salem's city council for a *long* time, and she's always been the chair for the Samhain festivities. We like her a lot.

Cindy, on the other hand, is a stick in the mud, who wants to be on this committee to ensure that said festivities aren't too scary for Cindy and her *delicate* friends.

I snort, and Breena sticks me in the ribs with her elbow.

"Ow!"

"We could do cauldrons," Lucy puts in. "Potion bottles, grimoires, tarot decks, astrology charts. There are a lot of things other than black cats we can use for décor."

"I'm not letting my kids go anywhere with tarot decks," Cindy informs Lucy.

"That's your right, and I think it's safe to say we

won't miss you," I reply with a bright smile. "Let's bring in Ouija boards, too."

"Now see here," Cindy begins, but Marydell raises her hands and tells us all to shut up.

"I may not be a witch," Marydell begins, glaring at Cindy, "but my friends are, and we will all be respectful to each other. If you can't do that, we don't need you on the committee. And that goes both ways."

Marydell aims her glare my way, and I sigh.

"I apologize for being disrespectful," I say dutifully.

"I'm leaving," Cindy announces, standing and slinging her purse over her shoulder. "Come on, Lacey."

"No way, I'm staying," Lacey Atwell says, shaking her head. "You're the one who has a problem with witches, which is a mystery to me since you live in Salem, Massachusetts."

"But we said we'd do this *together*," Cindy whines.

"I said I'd come with you. Not that I'd leave with you."

Cindy's mouth firms, and she aims a glare at all of us before storming off.

"Does anyone else have issues working alongside the other people in this group?" Marydell asks, looking around the room.

Everyone shakes their heads.

"Good. Now, back to the task at hand. I *like* the idea of tarot cards."

Chapter Four
Xander

"You need more soup." Breena's mom, Hilda, smiles at me as she ladles more steaming hot broccoli cheddar soup into my bowl while her sister, Astrid, passes me another slice of bread.

"I appreciate the food," I say after swallowing a bite of some of the best bread I've ever had in my life. "And the company of two beautiful women. But why am I here, ladies?"

"What a thing to ask," Astrid says, clucking her tongue on the roof of her mouth. "Why can't we simply ask a good friend to come over for lunch?"

"Our coven leader, no less," Hilda agrees, nodding.

"Of course, you can." I take a spoonful of soup, watching them as I swallow. They both have innocent smiles pasted on their faces.

And when I glance at the doorway of their cozy kitchen, I see Lucy's mom, Agatha, smiling at me, as well.

Which wouldn't be a big deal, except Agatha has been dead for two years.

Not that that keeps her from hanging out with her family.

"But I get the feeling that the three of you have something up your sleeves, and since I'm a psychic, I'm usually right about these kinds of things. Not to mention, you don't have poker faces."

"How are you?" Hilda asks, leaning in close to rest her hand on my arm. "How are you, *really*?"

"I'm...fine."

"That's not an answer," Astrid replies, shaking her head. "We worry about you, Xander. What you went through at Beltane was traumatic for everyone involved, so I can only imagine how horrible it was for you."

I blink and look down at the soup I'm suddenly no longer hungry for.

"Beltane is over."

"But is it?" Agatha asks from the doorway.

"You never talk," I reply, frowning at the ghost. "You just hover, slam doors, and scowl."

"I speak when it's needed."

"We're all worried about you," Astrid says again. "You're strong, Xander. Your powers are unlike anything I've ever seen in my life—and I've known many witches in my time. But you're also a man, and it will be good for you to talk about it."

"Talking about it is pointless."

How can I describe the absolute horror of those few

days? The agony of being torn apart from the inside out, of being manipulated into harming the one person who means more to me than anyone or anything in the universe.

The absolute terror of believing I'd killed her.

"It's not pointless," Hilda insists. "Our girl loves you, and we need to make sure you're okay. That you're healing from everything that happened."

"Your girl doesn't love me, not like that. Not like she once did."

"Oh, pishposh." Astrid flaps her hand around her head. "That's ridiculous. The girl is crazy about you. She's just stubborn."

You don't know what happened.

"We will always love each other, but that doesn't mean we can be together. And regarding everything at Beltane, well...I'm dealing with it."

"How?" Hilda demands. "How are you *dealing with it*, exactly?"

I'm avoiding it. I don't think about it, and I move on. Because we're not even close to being out of the woods yet, and I have too damn much to do.

"In my own way."

"Stubborn man," Astrid mutters and blows out a frustrated breath.

"I'm not really someone who wants to sit down and chat about my feelings. Even with you two."

A door slams somewhere in the house.

"Okay, you three."

"Well, you should." Hilda's smile is sweet and motherly. It's no wonder Breena is so sweet; she's just like her mother. "Because it usually helps a person to move on and heal from the thing that hurt them."

"Yeah, well, the thing that hurt me is still out there and is going to keep trying to hurt the people I care about. And on top of that, we have a curse to lift, and I just don't have time to wallow in self-pity."

"What are you talking about?" Astrid's voice is hard and all business now. "We all defeated that monster."

"We won a battle," I reply, dragging my hand down my face. "But it's not gone."

"When were you going to tell us?" Hilda asks.

"I'm calling a coven meeting for tomorrow night. Not only is it not dead, but it's also back. And I want everyone to be on high alert."

I glance over at Agatha. She has the saddest look on her face.

"What do you know?" I ask her.

She only shakes her head and leaves the room.

"About before—" Hilda begins, but I shake *my* head, stopping her from completing whatever she was about to say.

"There's no need to discuss it. Thank you for worrying about me, and for loving me. I love you both, too. But I'm fine. And this soup was amazing."

I wipe my mouth and stand from the table. I always feel so big in their small kitchen, but also very much at home.

Both women kiss me on the cheek before sending me on my way.

Rather than shifting into anything, I decide to walk in my human body for a while. It feels much different than the raven, wolf, or even the cat. And I like it.

I can smell the change of seasons in the air as I walk down the cracked and uneven sidewalk in Salem. The trees are just beginning to change, and there's a crispness to the air that wasn't there just a few days ago.

It makes me worry.

Time is passing so fast, and we're not ready for the battle I know is coming.

For *several* of the upcoming battles, now that I think about it.

The aunts—as Lorelei and her cousins refer to them —want me to talk about what happened during Beltane, but to tell them about it, to *really* delve into what happened and share that with them, would give them nightmares for the rest of their lives.

It's bad enough that I'll have to deal with it for the rest of mine. I don't intend to share that burden with anyone I care about.

Some days, I'm able to convince myself it was just a nightmare. That sitting in that abandoned house for days, caught in a web of light, pain, fear, and despair, didn't happen at all.

That I didn't stand over the love of my life, tie her down, and torture her. Murder her.

I would have lost her forever if not for the ward on the back of her neck.

But it did happen. Every agonizing moment of it happened, and at times, like now, each second of it replays in my head as if *it* can press the button on a machine and roll the film through my mind's eye.

Because reliving it, each and every time, is another moment of torture.

Wanting to see for myself that Lorelei is healthy and whole, I walk toward her cottage. As I stride down her driveway, I see her standing at the edge of the shoreline, staring out at the bay.

That's not unusual for her. She is a sea witch, after all.

But the way her hair blows back from her face when there is no wind to speak of makes the hair on the back of my neck stand on end. I pick up my pace, eager to get to her.

"Lora."

I say her name a couple of times, but she doesn't acknowledge me.

Finally, when I lay my hand on her shoulder, she blinks and turns to me, confusion in her pretty green eyes.

It's just like it was the other day when I approached her as the wolf.

"Oh, hi." She swallows and frowns. "Geez, I've been so nauseous lately. Every time I come close to the water. It's the weirdest thing."

"What were you looking at out there?"

"Huh?" She blinks up at me and then looks back out at the water. "Oh. I heard the music playing again. Did you hear it?"

"No." I watch her closely and brush her curly, auburn hair over her shoulder. "No, I didn't hear it."

"Odd. I've been hearing it a lot lately."

I don't like that. Not at all.

And I have some research to do before I talk to her about it because I'm afraid it'll just scare her, and Lorelei has been afraid enough to last a lifetime.

"What are you up to?" she asks.

"I just came from your mother and Hilda's house."

Her eyebrows lift in surprise. "Oh?"

"They invited me over for lunch. And wanted to grill me."

"About what?" She walks over to a fallen log and sits, gesturing for me to join her. So, I straddle the driftwood and face her.

"About Beltane. I guess they wanted to play therapists and make sure I'm doing okay."

"That sounds like them." Lorelei grins and nods her head slowly. "Yeah, that sounds exactly like something they'd do. What did you tell them?"

"That I'm fine."

She narrows her eyes, examining me. "And *are* you? Fine?"

I shrug a shoulder and look out at the harbor and the bay beyond. "I will be. Eventually. How are *you*?"

"Physically, I'm recovered from that day. Have been for a while now."

"Spiritually? Emotionally?"

She bites her lower lip and fiddles with a piece of tourmaline she's pulled from her pocket.

I'm glad she's carrying the protection stone with her.

"I'm still a little bruised, but I think that's to be expected. I suspect you're the same."

"Yeah." I scoot closer to her on the log and take her hand in mine, the tourmaline pressed between our palms. She stiffens at first but then relaxes and grips my hand in hers. "We're going to get through this. All of us. And once we're on the other side, this will all have been a really crappy year that we can be thankful to move on from."

"You think?"

"I know."

She tips her head up so she can look me in the eyes. "How do you know? How can you be sure?"

"I'm psychic, remember?"

A smile tickles the sides of her lips. "I am, too, and I can't see how this plays out. And trust me, that pisses me right off."

The truth is, neither can I, but my goal is to set her mind at ease...if only for a little while.

"Then just trust me. Everything will be fine."

"I'm psychic enough to know when you're placating me, but I'll play along for now."

"What are your plans for the rest of the day?" I ask her.

"I finished writing, so I was thinking I'd take some more things I gathered for the tapestry to Breena and then pop into the apothecary to get some vitamin K eye cream to help keep the crow's feet at bay. And I could use some more sleepytime tincture."

"You don't have any crow's feet."

She smirks. "Exactly. Vitamin K is a must. What are you doing today?"

"Whatever you're doing."

She sighs deeply. "You know, I've been pretty mean to you over the past couple of years."

"Yep."

"And yet, here you are, insisting on hanging out with me."

"Yep."

"Does that make you a masochist?"

"Nope."

She glances up at me, and I see there is no humor in her eyes. She's dead serious.

"I cannot leave you unprotected. That doesn't make you weak. And it doesn't make me an asshole."

"You didn't—" She swallows hard, then shakes her head and pulls away, tugging her hand out of mine.

"I didn't what?"

"Forget it. It doesn't matter. You wanna hang around? Fine. I won't stop you. But when all of this is over, Xander, you need to let me go."

My throat works on a swallow full of emotion. I don't *want* to let her go.

"You need to," she repeats. "Come on, I want to get to the apothecary before it closes."

"Wait." I grab her hand once more and lean in, then cup her cheek and watch as her pupils dilate and her bee-stung lips part in anticipation. "I won't ever let you go, Lorelei. I won't pressure you or bother you, but I won't ever get over you. It's impossible for me."

Those lips press together as she closes her eyes and exhales, and then she simply stands and walks toward her cottage.

My heart aches as I watch her walk away.

"Look at these new candles Breena made for my shop," Lucy says to Lorelei, holding up a glass container filled with wax, flowers, and crystals. Lorelei smells one and gushes over how pretty they are.

"I need one of each," Lorelei declares. "I want the amethyst, the aquamarine, *and* the rose quartz. But I can wait. I don't want to take them from customers."

"She's making me more," Lucy says with a grin as she sets the candles aside for her cousin. "I knew these would fly off the shelves."

"Awesome. I'm going to browse a bit."

"Please, do." Lucy turns to me with a wide smile and shrewd eyes. "And what can I get for you?"

"I'm not really in the market for anything."

"Everyone's in the market for something," she returns, tapping her finger on her chin, pondering. "Everyone needs a good moisturizer. Even men."

"Especially men," Lorelei calls out from across the room.

"Why *especially* men?" I ask.

"Because they *never* use it. Skin is skin."

I glance back at Lucy, who's covering a laugh with her hand.

"I have a nice men's skincare line," Lucy continues as she reaches for a little pot of something.

"How is it different from the women's line?"

"The smell," she says with a grin. "It has notes of cedar and tobacco with just a hint of sage, and we all know that sage is very protective. You can't go wrong with it."

"I'm about to buy face cream," I mutter, staring down at the amber-colored pot with the black lid.

"You need beard oil, too. The scent is the same."

"I don't have a beard."

"Sometimes, you have scruff. This will make it softer."

"Why do I think you're just trying to sell me more stuff?"

"I own a shop," Lucy says with a shrug, and I hear

Lorelei laugh from behind a shelf full of more bottles. "Do you do spell work?"

"Of course, I do."

"Well, let me know if you need some herbs." She gestures to the wall with floor-to-ceiling shelves stacked with huge jars full of every herb you can think of. I know she grew them all right here on the property.

Lorelei comes walking up to the checkout counter with her arms full of things she intends to buy.

"You have so much new stuff," Lorelei says. "I love it. And I need everything. Where's Jonas?"

"He's in Hallows End for a few hours."

I look in the direction where the town that's stuck in the year 1692 lies, even though I know I can't see it.

"Does he go every day?" I ask her.

"He tries to. He needs the townspeople to see him and has to make sure that nothing weird is going on there. So far, at least recently, there haven't been any changes in anything."

"Good. For now, until we lift the damn curse, that's good."

"I agree. He'll be headed back soon, I'm sure. Did you want to see him?"

"I have a few questions for him, but it's nothing urgent. How much do I owe you?"

"Sixty-seven fifty."

I blink at her. "For *face cream*?"

"And oil. Beauty is expensive." Lucy grins and simply waits for me to pull my wallet out of my pocket.

"I'll just remind myself that I'm supporting a small business," I mutter, handing her my credit card. Lucy charges my new purchases to it, then stows the cream and oil in a plain brown paper bag with handles, before tossing in a small stone and some stickers.

"What was that for?"

"Freebies," Lucy says. "My little gift to you as a thank-you. I'll put yours on your tab, Lorelei."

"Thanks." Lorelei claps her hands in excitement as her cousin carefully packs her treasures in a bag of her own. "I'm so excited about all of this. I'm going to start burning that money candle *today*."

"Are you running out of money?" I ask her.

"A girl can always use a little extra cash." Lorelei winks at Lucy and takes her bag. "You know, the other day at the committee meeting, when you mentioned tarot cards, it reminded me that I haven't worked with tarot in a long while. I used to love it, and I want to get back into the practice. Do you want to get together so we can read each other?"

"Sounds fun," Lucy says with a nod. "I have a new deck to work with, too."

"I found my old one," Lorelei replies. "I have so many, but I love this old one. My connection to it is really cool."

"I love when that happens," Lucy replies, glancing at me. "Do you read tarot?"

"I haven't in a long time."

"I'd love to read your cards," Lucy says. "We definitely need to do this soon. In the meantime, I'll start practicing again."

"Me, too." Lorelei smiles. "I'm going back to drawing a card every day. It's a nice routine. Okay, thanks for the loot. I'll see you later."

"See you," Lucy says with a wave. I follow Lorelei out the door and down to her waiting car.

"I'll see you later," I say, leaning on the window of her car after she climbs inside. "I have some things to see to. Please, be safe."

"I'll be fine," she assures me. "Honest. Stop worrying so much."

She winks at me, starts the car, then drives off.

I walk the half mile or so to my home, unlock the door, and walk inside. It smells a little musty because I haven't been home much this past week, so I flick my finger at the windows, and all of them open to let in some fresh air.

I thumb through my mail and trash it all when I see it's just junk, then walk up the stairs to my bedroom and bathroom.

I need a shower and a change of clothes.

And I need to cast a few spells to strengthen my protective barriers for both me and my home.

When I step out of the shower and sling the towel around my waist, I walk to the sink and wipe the fog off the glass with another towel, feeling a seed of anger plant itself in my gut.

"You're not fucking real."

It doesn't reply. It just grins.

It doesn't have a form. Not human, anyway. It's mist —swirling blue and purple mist—and when I begin to speak, the haunting, weird face in the center of it scowls in rage.

"Visions in glass, trickery of eye, be gone from this place, leave from my mind. I banish this evil, evict what I see, this is my will, so mote it be."

The scream doesn't surprise me this time. And then, it's gone.

I stand very still and listen, reaching out through my house with my mind, but it's empty. Even the little house spirit that sometimes shows up is gone.

I quickly dress and use the cream I just bought from Lucy on my face. I actually really like the smell of it, and the sage will be an added layer of protection.

I flick my fingers, and all the windows in the house close. I gather up the crystals I have placed throughout the house and set them in a selenite bowl for cleansing, and then I move to a drawer where I have fresh, cleansed and charged ones waiting for me, and place them in the four corners of the house.

Calling in the elements—Earth, Fire, Water, and Air —I work a protection spell that will keep my home safe while I'm gone.

I use oils and powders on my skin and hair, rein-forcing the protection spells on myself, and then slip a leather cord over my head. A large piece of powerfully spelled obsidian hangs from it.

With other crystals in my pockets, I lock the door behind me and just step onto the sidewalk when my phone rings.

"What's up, Lucy?"

"Hurry, Lorelei's been hurt."

CHAPTER FIVE
LORELEI

"**Y**ou should have gone to the hospital."

I roll my eyes at my mother just as Xander comes storming through my front door, his expression mutinous and tension in every line of his impressive body.

"Where is she?"

"It's not a big house," I reply, cringing when my split lip stings from talking. "I'm right here."

"Here's some ice for that fat lip," Lucy says, passing me an ice pack.

"Thanks."

"What the fuck happened?" Xander demands as he kneels before me and tips my chin up with his finger, taking me in.

"It looks worse than it is," I inform him and wince when my lip cracks again.

"I think you should tell us all what happened," Jonas prompts from across the room.

I glance around and see everyone staring at me like I might break at any moment.

"Okay, it was creepy." I take a deep breath and ignore the throbbing headache setting up residence behind my eyes.

"Wait, this will help," Jonas says, then walks to me, wraps his big hands around my head at the temples, and whispers something I can barely hear. When he's finished, my headache is gone.

"It's really handy having a healer in the family."

Jonas smiles softly and leans in to kiss my forehead before stepping back to his wife.

"Okay, spill," Breena says.

"I was driving home from Lucy's, happy with my new finds and just minding my own business when that creepy-as-hell red dog with the human eyes came walking right out into the street all of a sudden and then just stood there. And I was like, no way on Gaia's green Earth are you going to mess with me today, you smarmy bastard. So, I kept going, intending to kill the little son of a bitch, but then it just sort of...melted into a puddle of water, and my car hydroplaned off the road and into a telephone pole."

I shake my head mournfully.

"Now I have to get a new car, and that one was just fine."

"Yes, let's all mourn the car," Giles replies, sarcasm dripping from his voice.

"I liked it," I say with a scowl. "I got a little beat up, but it's nothing serious. Called a tow truck, but someone must have been looking on because an ambulance and a fire truck both showed up before the tow did."

"I wasn't at home that long," Xander says with a scowl.

"It's been about two hours," I reply softly. "And, no, it's not your fault."

Xander looks stricken. "I took a fifteen-minute shower, got dressed, and freshened my protection spells around the house. It was no more than an hour."

Then he blinks and shakes his head.

"What is it?"

"I saw *it* in the mirror after my shower. I thought it lasted all of two minutes—if that."

"It was holding you there while it fucked with Lorelei," Giles guesses.

I look around my small living room. My mom and Aunt Hilda are here, along with my cousins, their men, and Xander.

I was relieved that I didn't have to be alone when they all showed up, but it wasn't until Xander arrived that my heart started to calm down. It's like he's a Xanax for my soul, and that's incredibly irritating.

"Why didn't you go to the hospital?" Xander asks, still kneeling next to me. I have a feeling that if I'd allow it, he'd scoop me up and set me on his lap.

"Because I'm *fine*. I have some bumps and bruises, and I'm pissed off, but I don't need a hospital. Jonas is our healer, and I know Lucy will have something, too. There's no need to be dramatic."

"Right, a psychotic *being* is fucking with you, runs you off the road, and there's no need to be dramatic," Xander says, nodding.

Xander is *never* sarcastic. It's just not in his nature.

"Okay," Mom says, jumping in. "I think everyone needs to take a deep breath. Lorelei, Jonas *will* take a good look at you, and if he thinks you need a hospital, you'll go, and that's all there is to it."

"She's okay," Jonas says, smiling at me. "Time will heal her, along with some witch hazel and arnica."

"See?" I point to Jonas triumphantly. "I'm just *fine*. You can all go home."

"I'm not going anywhere," Xander replies, shaking his head. "Not a chance."

"I don't need to be babysat—"

"Do you think I'd *leave*?" he demands, fire flashing in his black eyes. "That I'd just walk out that door, knowing you're hurting?"

"That's what you do!" I explode as pure fury rolls through me. "You fucking *leave me* when I need you the most! So don't sit there and act like you want to stay and protect me now that the stakes are high because it wasn't that long ago that I *begged* you not to go, and you just sauntered right out anyway. And the stakes were *much* higher than this time, and you know it."

Xander and I are panting heavily, glaring at each other, and the room is deadly quiet.

"What happened?" Jonas asks gently. It immediately brings tears to my eyes, but I don't look away from Xander. He's not angry now, he's sad and grieving, and I want to both slap him and wrap him up in my arms.

"Tell them," he says. "You need to."

I shake my head and cover my face with my hands. I don't want to speak of it; because if I do, it'll be true, and the utter grief will just tear me apart all over again.

But after everything we've been through as a family, and all we still have to endure, they deserve to know what kind of a broken woman I am.

"Baby, please talk to us." My mom strokes her hand down my hair soothingly, and I want to sob.

So, I do.

Mom gathers me close, and I cry into her shoulder, letting out a lot of the grief I thought I'd processed over the past two years while I was away.

Someone covers me with a blanket. Someone else wipes my face with a cool, wet washcloth.

Finally, after the crying jag, I blow my nose and sit up, looking around the room.

Xander has walked over to stare out my windows at the water, his hands shoved into his pockets, looking so tall and strong...and so weary.

Everyone else just watches and waits.

Breena's already dabbing at her tears. She's such a

gifted empath that when someone feels big emotions around her, she feels them, too.

Goddess, I love her.

I love them all, even the one who caused this.

"A few years ago, maybe three months before I left for California, I was pregnant."

Breena gasps, and my mom takes my hand.

"Xander and I decided to wait until we got through the first trimester to tell everyone, just in case. You know, how some people do. I know my mom lost a baby before me, and I just wanted to make sure everything was on track before we announced it to the family."

Xander's back twitches in agitation.

"I had a bad dream. We were a few days away from telling all of you and planned to announce it at the Yule party the aunts always throw for the family. I even made fun T-shirts for them. We were really excited. But I had a bad dream, and it just stuck with me."

I glance at Xander again, and he turns from the window to look at me. His face is hard, but his expression isn't guarded.

Still, his eyes are so damn sad.

"I was fourteen weeks along. Xander had to go out on his boat to work that day, and I asked him not to go. And then the feeling just got stronger and stronger."

I have to stop because my voice cracks, and then I wipe a tear away from my eye.

"Something was so *wrong*. I'd been to the doctor the day before, and everything was fine, but I knew in my gut that it wasn't. As the feeling grew stronger, I started begging Xander. '*Please* don't go to work. Stay with me. I think something's wrong.'"

I shake my head and dab at more tears.

"I'd been really emotional throughout the pregnancy —more than usual—and I'm sure he thought I was being dramatic. But I didn't care. I needed him to stay."

"And I didn't."

All eyes turn to Xander when he speaks up.

"I didn't believe that anything was wrong. We'd been to the doctor, got a clean bill of health, and I'm fucking psychic. I didn't see anything wrong. I had to make the run-out. It was the last one before the holidays, and my crew depended on that money for their families. So, I kissed Lora goodbye, told her not to worry, and left."

"Oh, shit," Giles says, dragging his hand down his face.

"I was so scared," I whisper. "And so *mad*. So freaking mad. For the first half of the day, nothing happened. So, I began thinking maybe I really was just being super dramatic, that it had simply been a stupid dream, and I'd be fine. I even had myself talked into that being the case, and although I was still peeved at Xander, I wasn't as mad as I had been that morning.

"But then, around lunchtime, I was in the kitchen deciding if I wanted a sandwich or a salad when it suddenly felt like someone stabbed me in the stomach. I was doubled over in pain and couldn't catch my breath. I tried to call Xander, but he didn't have a signal out where he was. So, I called my doctor. He had an ambulance come get me and then met me at the hospital. But it was too late by the time I got there. There was no heartbeat."

I blow my nose again.

"I was told I could naturally miscarry on my own, or they could do a procedure to take care of it there and then. All I wanted was Xander. It didn't even occur to me that I should call anyone else—and I don't mean for that to hurt anyone's feelings. I wasn't thinking, and—"

"It's okay," Mom says with a nod. "We understand what you mean."

I blow out a breath and wipe my nose again. It's sore from hitting the pole with my car and all the wiping, but I ignore it and finish my story.

"Our baby died in that hospital room, and I was all alone. I tried to be rational for a while and work through the anger and hurt, but I just couldn't. It broke me, and it broke my relationship with Xander because how could I trust that when things hit the fan, I could depend on him?"

"That's not fair," Aunt Hilda says, shaking her head slowly. She wipes at a tear but continues talking. "My darling child, it wasn't Xander's fault you lost your sweet babe. It wasn't his doing."

"No, but he didn't listen to me."

"I made the most terrible mistake of my life," Xander says, his voice rough and full of regret. "And if you think it doesn't replay in my head every day, you're wrong. I apologized. I grieved with you. I did everything I knew how to do after the fact."

"But it wasn't good enough." Finished with tears, I take the blanket off my lap and set it aside. "Because you didn't give me what I truly needed."

"That's bullshit." This comes from Lucy, who's glaring at me with hot green eyes. "That's just pure bullshit, Lorelei. You've been punishing Xander for the death of your child for *years* because you need someone to blame, and he's the easiest target. The truth is, there isn't anyone to blame. He had a job to do, and with the information he had available to him, he thought it was safe to do it. I think most people would make the same decision."

"But—"

"I'm not finished. You could have turned to any of the four women looking at you right now or my mom because she was still living at the time, and all of us would have dropped whatever we were doing to be with you. Saying it didn't occur to you is a cop-out. You *wanted* to blame Xander. You've basically been throwing a temper tantrum for almost three years, and that's just ridiculous."

"That's enough," Jonas says, taking his wife's shoulders in his hands from behind. "You're angry, and—"

"You're damn right, I'm angry. We've been asking you for years what happened, and you always blow us off. This is a big fucking deal. The *biggest*. And rather than let us help you through it, you kept it a secret, punished

Xander, and ran away. If anyone in this room runs at the first sign of trouble, it's *you*, Lorelei. Xander tried to make it right, but you moved all the way to California. You know what? I'm out."

Lucy stomps to the door, whips it open, and storms out without a backward glance. Jonas sighs, crosses to me, and kisses my cheek. "Blessed be."

He follows behind Lucy.

"I'm mad, too," Breena admits softly. "But more than that, I'm hurt that you've carried this burden all on your own and didn't let any of us help. We would have helped you, Lorelei. You're our sister. I'm so sorry for your loss. The loss for all of us. That baby is so loved, even now."

With that, Breena stands and takes Giles's hand.

"I think we'd better go," he says, and they leave, as well.

"Are you going to yell at me, too?" I ask my mom and Aunt Hilda.

"Thought about it," Mom says but then shakes her head. "You're my strong-willed, stubborn girl, and nothing you do surprises me anymore. But you've never been the kind to deny when you're wrong. Or to punish others, especially those you love."

I blink away fresh tears and watch as Xander turns back to look outside once more.

"What you went through was just horrible," Aunt Hilda adds. "A tragedy in every sense of the word. And you're still suffering through it, to this day. Punishing

Xander, and in turn yourself, hasn't helped you heal, darling. That's not the way. But you already know that."

"I'm scared," I whisper and close my eyes.

"There's no need," Mom says softly and kisses my cheek. "Hilda, we have some bread dough rising we need to see to."

"You're right. Let's go do that."

I open my eyes and watch as Mom and Aunt Hilda leave, and then I take a breath and simply hold Xander's gaze as he sits in the chair opposite mine.

"I don't know what to do next," I admit.

He doesn't answer for a long time. He just sits and watches me. When I see tears form in his gorgeous dark eyes, I can't help myself from crossing to him, climbing into his lap, wrapping my arms around him, and burying my face in his neck.

He clings to me.

His hands and arms are so strong, and he's usually careful with me because he knows how strong he is, but right now, those arms and hands clutch me tightly. I hear the breath catching in his lungs.

"I'm sorry." I pull back to allow him room to bury *his* face in *my* neck so I can console him. It never occurred to me until right now that I never allowed us to grieve. We might have lived in the same house for a while after the fact, but I never allowed us a moment to be vulnerable and sad together.

I was just too mad.

And part of me is still angry. But I can't stand seeing the hurt and not do something to comfort him.

"I didn't know," he whispers, and I can feel his hot tears on my neck. "I truly didn't know, baby. I never would have left you that day if—"

"Okay." I take his face in my hands and wipe away his tears with my thumbs. "I know you wouldn't have gone if you'd known."

"But *you* did know, and that's been the point all along."

I close my eyes and nod, but then it's as if a door has been opened, and all the resentment and anger just washes right out of it.

Because now, *finally*, he understands.

"It wasn't all on you. Not the way the girls made it sound," Xander says, brushing a piece of my hair off my face and tucking it behind my ear. "I was guarded, too. Defensive. Angry. I thought I was trying to make things right, but I didn't try that hard. I didn't know what to do with you. You wouldn't even look at me."

"I know. I couldn't. I felt so guilty and ashamed."

"Whoa." He lifts my chin with his finger and frowns at me. "Why would you feel like that?"

"Because I lost our baby, and I knew how much we wanted it. I thought that I must have done something wrong."

"You didn't," he insists. "I heard the doctor myself. He said things like that just happen sometimes, Lorelei."

"Yeah, well, I didn't believe him."

"Do you believe it now?"

"I want to say I do, but I don't know. I look back on that time and wonder if I drank too much caffeine, or—"

"You didn't do anything wrong." He lets his fingertips drag down my cheek, and it just feels so damn good, I can't help but lean in to his touch. "And neither did I."

I pause because I want to argue. I still think he should have listened to me that day.

But arguing won't change anything.

And for the first time in almost three years, I feel at peace.

"I think I need a nap." I let my eyes drift closed. "Between the fender bender and the crying jag, I'm really tired."

"We need to discuss your definition of a *fender bender*. But yeah, you nap." He settles me against him and kisses the top of my head. "And I'll be right here when you wake up."

Chapter Six
Xander

Lorelei's breathing has evened out, and I feel the tension has finally left her body as I cradle her in my lap. Yet even in sleep, she clings to me as if seeking protection.

It's been years since I sat with her like this, since she let her guard down with me at all, let alone enough to trust me to keep her safe when she's vulnerable like this. I would do this for a year if I could. Why can't time be extended for something like *this* rather than when I'm standing in my stupid bathroom, banishing the son of a bitch who's trying to kill us?

Because it wanted to keep me *away* from her.

She'll put up a fight, but I won't spend a night away from her again until all of this is resolved.

Hell, if I have my way, I won't spend another night away from her *period*.

Because she's mine, in every sense of the word, and she always has been. We're fated, but more than that, I'm so fucking in love with her I can't see straight. I love the way she isn't afraid to try new things. Her bluntness can be a little much for some, but I like that I never have to guess how she's feeling. She doesn't cover up the way she feels with a fake smile, and I appreciate that.

I love how much she adores her family and how fiercely protective she is of them.

But, at the heart of it, is the soul-deep connection I've always felt with her. I'm a few years older, but I've known Lorelei all her life. Once we both crossed over into puberty, I knew without a doubt that we were fated. There will never be anyone else for me.

As I told her earlier, I know I made the biggest mistake of my life, but damn it, I will make it up to her, and we'll resolve our past and heal together so we can move forward with our lives.

I just have to talk her into it.

With a gusty breath, I tip my head back and close my eyes. I feel like I've been hit by a metaphorical bus. Hearing Lorelei tell her family the story of what happened, and reliving all those emotions, felt like taking punches from someone much stronger than me. I think about our baby—and Lorelei—every single day of my life, wondering what our lives would be like now if we hadn't lost our child. I don't let myself dwell there, but I *do* think of it.

And, goddess, how I miss Lorelei. Whether she's in California or here in this cottage, it doesn't matter. She's part of me, and she was just...*gone*.

For the first time since the day she walked out on me, I feel some hope taking root, and I'm going to make sure those roots grow.

The wind outside is frantic. Was there supposed to be a storm blowing in? I make a habit of watching the weather constantly, all through the day, because it can change on a dime, and my livelihood depends on calmer seas.

I hadn't heard anything about this storm.

A tree branch knocks against the window behind the chair where I'm holding Lorelei. I can hear the rain tapping against the shingles on the roof above.

Storms like these usually move in and out fairly quickly, and as long as I'm on shore, I like to listen to them.

Add in the fact that I have Lorelei here on my lap, and it makes listening to the storm all the better.

Lorelei shifts to get more comfortable, and I pat her back soothingly.

"Don't want to lose it," she mutters in her sleep, rubbing her hands over her round belly. I lay one of mine over hers, feeling the baby move, healthy and strong inside her. Goddess, I adore them so much. It's shocking that my heart doesn't burst right out of me.

"Everything's fine," I assure her softly before gently kissing her head. "The doctor said the baby is healthy. There's nothing to worry about, my love."

Pleased that Lorelei seems to have drifted back to sleep, I rock in the chair and listen to the storm. Suddenly, the wind blows the front door open, slamming it violently against the wall, and lightning streaks across the sky like creepy little fingers. All of a sudden, I can hear a baby crying from the back bedroom.

"Lorelei, wake up. We have to see to the baby. The storm is scaring her, honey, and I need to get the door. Lora."

But instead of getting off my lap, she looks up at me with stark, white eyes.

"Shit. This is a nightmare."

The baby's cries grow louder—the child wailing as if someone's torturing her.

"You have no power here," I begin, my voice loud and strong. "Remove this menace, remove this blight, cast out this evil this very night. Free us from its wicked grasp, open the way, let goodness last. Cleanse this place and all within. We will prevail, it will not win."

"Xander."

I can hear Lorelei's voice, but the Lora in my lap isn't saying anything.

"Xander, wake up."

I suck in a quick breath. When I open my eyes, Lorelei has moved to straddle me and has my face between her sweet hands as she scowls down at me with concern.

"Hey," she says, stroking one hand down my cheek. "You were dreaming."

"Nightmare," I mutter, shaking my head. "Sorry."

"Don't be sorry." Sensing that I need to stand, she wiggles herself off my lap and steps away while I climb to my feet and move to stare out the window. There's no storm. The sun hasn't quite set yet, and the water looks calm. "Do you want to talk about it?"

Still hearing the baby's cries echoing in my ears, I shake my head and turn to look at her. "No. It was just a silly dream. I'm sorry I woke you up."

"I probably shouldn't have slept for so long anyway, not if I want to sleep tonight." She licks her lips. "Do you want to stay for dinner? I can whip something up."

I wouldn't say no if my life depended on it.

"Sure. I should go do my evening patrol really quick and make sure the others are okay. Do I have time for that? Will you be okay here for less than thirty minutes?"

"Of course. I'll be fine. You go fly or do whatever it is you do, and I'll get dinner going."

"I won't be long," I promise and move to the door.

"Xander?"

I stop and look back at her, finding her watching me with concern still written all over her gorgeous face.

"Are you sure you're okay?"

"Yeah. I'm fine. I'll be back soon."

I want to pull her into my arms and take comfort in her, but instead, I head out to do my rounds, needing some time to clear my head.

I do this a few times a day since *it* has decided to dick with us again. I shift into the raven and fly around Salem, checking to see that everything is as it should be, and then I fly to Lucy and Jonas's place, and then to Giles and Breena's. I want to be sure they're safe.

The raven has always been the easiest for me to shift into. It was the first form I discovered as a kid, much to my mom's dismay. I come from a long, long line of witches, so the shifting in and of itself didn't scare her, but she didn't want me flying around on a whim. She worried about me.

She still does and calls me often. She and my grandmother have insisted that they travel from their retirement community in Florida up to Salem for Samhain this year.

I would rather they stayed down south where they're safe, but when I said as much, they wouldn't have it. And, selfishly, I'm excited to see them in a few weeks.

So, with the wind blowing around me, I soar over the little city I love so much. Tourists walk down cobblestone streets, some wearing the black witches' hats sold all over town. I see two separate walking tours with more tourists listening raptly as the guide tells stories of people who have been gone for centuries.

Marydell Roberts stands in front of the city hall, holding a briefcase as she chats with our mayor, Albert Kinney. The conversation seems heated, at least based on how Marydell firms her lips into a fine line.

Pleased that everything in town seems to be in order, I first fly over to my home, seeing that it's just as I left it earlier today, then head to Giles and Breena's house.

From the outside, all looks well. When I reach in with my mind, only allowed to do so because I made arrangements with Giles several weeks ago, I can see that everything is calm. Breena works at her loom, and Giles reads in a chair nearby.

I leave to fly over Breena's former house—the one she abandoned after *it* tried to kill her last Samhain—and narrow my eyes.

I sense water in the house.

I'll have to tell Breena we need to check it out.

Finally, I circle over to Lucy's apothecary, where she and Jonas also live. Again, all is calm on the outside, but when I reach in, I see that Lucy is still upset from earlier. She's pacing, talking to herself, and feeling hurt.

Incredibly hurt.

Jonas stands out back in the gardens, his hands on his hips as he stares toward Hallows End. I can't read his mind, but I can tell he's thinking about the town he spent more than three hundred years in and worrying about setting it free.

While I hate that both of my friends are struggling, there's nothing I can do to help them. Content that they're at least safe, I turn to fly back to Lorelei.

The sun has just set as the roof of the cottage comes into view, and I'm surprised to see that Lorelei is standing outside, just a few steps from the porch, her arms wrapped around herself as she stares out at the harbor and bay.

I land, shift back into my human form, and walk to

her. Her eyes are wide and unblinking, and I don't like it one bit.

"Lorelei."

She doesn't respond; she just continues to stare out at the water.

"Hey, Lorelei." This time, I reach out and lay my hand on her shoulder. She jerks as if I've pulled her out of a trance and then stares up at me, blinking quickly. "You were deep in thought."

"I was? Oh." She frowns and glances back out at the water. "Why do I always hear that music?"

"What does it sound like?"

"It's just so...*pretty*. Unlike anything I've ever heard before. And I feel so good when I listen to it. Like I'm floating or something. But then, whenever it goes away, I feel *awful*."

"Come on, let's go inside."

I take her hand, and she doesn't pull away, which I take as a good sign. Leading her through the front door, I close it behind us.

"See? Once I'm back in the cottage, I'm fine." She frowns up at me. "But the closer I get to the water, the sicker I feel."

"How long has this been going on?"

She walks into the kitchen and opens the oven, checking on whatever smells so good inside.

"I don't know. A few weeks, I guess? Since the day you approached me as the wolf."

"You hadn't heard it before that?"

"Not that I remember." She pulls a big, round stone out of the oven, and a pizza sizzles on top of it. "I didn't put anchovies on this."

"I'll eat just about anything."

"I know." She pulls a pizza cutter out of a drawer, quickly divides the pie into eight slices, then tosses the utensil into the sink. "I can make a salad with this if you want."

"I think the pizza is plenty."

She nods. "That's what I thought, too. It's comfort food, you know? And I thought we could both use it."

"You're right."

She glances at me with those gorgeous green eyes as if she's nervous, then sets a few slices onto a plate and passes it to me before dishing up her own.

"Let's sit in the living room." She leads me into the other room and sits cross-legged on the couch while I take the same chair I occupied earlier while cradling her against me.

"This chair doesn't rock." I frown, looking down at it.

"Nope. Why do you look surprised?"

"It rocked in my dream." I shake my head, take a bite of the pizza, and then stare at Lorelei in disbelief.

"Did I ruin it?" she demands.

"Hell, no. This is amazing." I swallow and take another bite. "We're never ordering out again. This is far and away better than anything we can buy around here."

Her cheeks flush with happiness as she takes a bite of

her own slice. "I guess if this whole witchy author thing doesn't work out, I could open a pizza kitchen."

"No. I'm keeping this secret all to myself."

"I can't even tell the cousins?"

I chew, contemplating. "Maybe. *Maybe* it's okay if they know, but they have to sign a contract that they won't tell anyone else."

She giggles and shakes her head. "Now you're just being silly, and you're never silly."

"I have moments. With you."

Her laugh softens into a smile, and she studies me, her plate of pizza resting on her lap.

"You should eat."

"I will," she replies and then looks down at her slice, but she doesn't take a bite. "I've been thinking since you left to go out on patrol. I hurt everybody I love the most today. Have been hurting them for a long time."

"They felt hurt because they would have helped you." I continue to eat the glorious pizza. "They would have wanted you to lean on them."

"I know." Her response is a whisper. "And I'm a shit because Lucy's right. I didn't call on them because I needed to be mad at you. To take everything out on you and wrap my sorrow, anger, and fear around me like a stupid blanket. I really did throw a temper tantrum, and I don't like knowing that."

"Lorelei." I set my plate aside and lean forward, my elbows on my knees. "You're a human being, so you need to give yourself a little grace here. You...*we* lost a baby. No one is prepared for that or knows how to deal with it. There's no instruction manual. Directing your anger at me was probably the most natural thing to do. Hell, I did the same. I just never said anything."

"Because I'm the mean one."

"Okay, stop feeling sorry for yourself." She narrows her eyes at me, and I grin. "Do you have a mean streak? Yes, Lorelei, you always have. I don't know what it says about me that your sassiness is one of the things I love most about you. I think you and I went through quite possibly the most difficult thing a couple can go through. We lost a child. Even if that baby was still tiny, we didn't love it any less."

"No, we didn't." She exhales and takes a bite of her pizza. "I clung to my anger toward you so tightly. Honestly, I feel kind of naked now that I'm working through it. And that makes me feel vulnerable, and I don't like it."

"I know." I follow her lead and go back to eating my pizza. "I want nothing more than to work through this with you."

"We can't be together." She slices her hand through the air. "Absolutely not."

"Why not, exactly?"

"Trust, for one."

"Are you really going to sit there and tell me you don't trust me? That, deep down in your heart, you really think I'm untrustworthy? Come on, baby, you know that's not true."

"It was true. Once," she whispers. "I've lived the past several years severing myself from you."

"Didn't work."

"I turned off my emotions when it came to you. After a while, it wasn't anger I felt, but nothing at all. I was numb."

"Bullshit."

Her eyes flash at me, and I grin.

"See? That look, right there. The one that says, *I'm going to kick your ass.* That's not numbness, and you've given me that look from the moment you moved home and saw me at that first coven meeting with Jonas. You're not indifferent when it comes to me."

"It would be easier if I were." She finishes her pizza and sets the plate aside. "Besides, we have enough to deal with right now. We don't need to bring our feelings for each other into the mix."

"Maybe we do." I shake my head when she starts to argue. "I think the bonds that tie us all together only make us stronger—as both witches and humans. If we strengthen those bonds, we'll have an even better chance of defeating the asshole and lifting the curse. We're powerful together, Lorelei."

"We're just as powerful as friends."

"No." I hold her gaze with mine. "We're not. And you know it."

Rather than reply, she stands and gathers our plates, then hurries into the kitchen and begins loading the dishwasher.

"I *refuse* to start up a relationship with you just because of some creep and a curse." She scowls down at the dishwasher tab in her hand before putting it into the compartment and slamming the door shut. "That's ridiculous."

I turn her around and cage her against the countertop. Goddess, she seems so tiny next to me. Always has.

"Do you think that's all this is? Do you honestly believe that the only reason I want you is because of the drama going on in our lives? For fuck's sake, Lorelei. I've loved you for my entire godsdamn life. My heart only beats because I know you're in this world, and I spend every moment of every day wishing for *you*."

"Xander—"

I tip her chin up when she moves to look away.

"I know we have a long journey ahead of us full of healing and learning. I'm not stupid. We can't pick up where we left off. But damn it, I want to try to make this work. I need you."

A single tear slips down her cheek, and I catch it with my finger.

"You can stay here," she says at last, then swallows. "I know it's safer for us to be together. You'll sleep in the guest room, though."

I smile. "That's a start."

"It's all I'm willing to give right now."

"I understand." I lean down and press my lips to her forehead, then step back and give her space. "Thank you."

She nods and blows out a breath. "This could be a huge mistake."

"Or the best thing ever."

"I guess there's no in-between, is there?"

I shrug a shoulder. "I don't see one."

"I have to make things right with my cousins."

"And you will. Tomorrow."

She nods and bites her lip. "Do you need to go get anything from your place?"

"I'll do that tomorrow, too."

"Okay, well, I'll show you to your room, then." She walks around me and down the hall that leads to the bedrooms, then opens the first door.

I feel my eyebrows climb into my hairline.

"That's a *twin* bed."

"I know." She covers a laugh with her hand. "I'm sorry, it's all I have. I don't have any other friends who are almost seven feet tall."

"You want me to sleep in *that*."

"It's all I have," she says again.

Without a word, I walk around her and open the door to her bedroom, seeing the California King bed in the middle of the room. Then, I turn back to her and raise an eyebrow.

"That's *my* bed," she says, propping her hands on her hips. "I told you. You have to sleep in the guest room."

"Then we'll swap the beds because that twin won't even accommodate one leg."

"Not my problem."

I narrow my eyes at her. "Wanna bet?"

CHAPTER SEVEN

He does so enjoy the torment. He didn't realize just how much. In the past, it was short-lived and followed quickly by the main event.

Death.

That is what he does all of this for. It fuels him. Drives him.

It brings him immense joy.

But the long-lasting misery and suffering he's been able to inflict on these little playthings has been *fun*.

And that's something he hasn't taken the time to indulge in for centuries.

It's become addicting for him.

From the safety of the water, he can see her as she walks along the shoreline, looking for her ridiculous trinkets. And when she bends over to pick up a shell, he smiles to himself.

He might have missed out on the kill last time—something that still fills him with unimaginable rage—but he won't fail again.

This little sea witch will get what's coming to her.

They all will.

CHAPTER EIGHT
LORELEI

I'm nervous.

I blow out a breath and busy myself making up the small twin bed in the guest room. I caved and gave Xander the king. As funny as it would have been to me, I just couldn't bring myself to make him suffer on the smaller bed.

Which, in all reality, is a major improvement from how I felt about him just a couple of months ago. Seems I'm growing as a person.

I smirk and, with the bed made, walk out to the kitchen where the man himself is standing at the sink, just finishing with the dishwasher.

In the three days he's lived here, I haven't done one dirty dish. It's as though he's decided to earn his keep around here. And honestly, I won't complain.

Even if he loads the dishwasher like a feral squirrel.

They'll get clean, and that's all that matters.

"I could have done that."

Xander doesn't even look my way as he wipes down the countertop. "I don't mind. You do most of the cooking, so it just makes sense that I clean."

"I'm not going to argue that point."

When I move to walk over and pour myself some coffee, Xander beats me to it. I watch, amused, as he doctors the brew just the way I would, then sets the spoon to stirring on its own before passing me the mug.

"Thanks. Are you trying to soften me up for something?" I sit on a stool at the end of the peninsula, pull my legs up under me, and sip my coffee. "Because you've been doing nice things like this all week."

"Maybe I'm just a nice guy."

He still doesn't look my way, and his face holds no trace of humor.

"Well, you typically *are* kind. Nice? No. Also, something's on your mind. Tell me."

He shakes his head, but when I don't back down or say anything else, he lets out a breath and tosses the rag into the sink before turning to me and leaning on the countertop across from me.

"Listen, I know we weren't together, and it's absolutely none of my business..."

I narrow my eyes in thought. "Okay."

"And I'm not going through your stuff."

"If I thought you were, you wouldn't be staying here. Not that I have anything to hide."

His lips twitch into a smile, but it's not happy or humor-filled.

"I happened to see your to-do list on your night-stand, and you made yourself a note to call Brian. And, well..." He blows out a breath and pushes his hand through his long, black-as-night hair in agitation. "Who the fuck is Brian?"

"Are you jealous?" I tilt my head to the side, watching in fascination. It's a stupid question. He's practically green.

But he doesn't answer. He just stares at me with those intense black eyes. The old me would have told him to mind his own fucking business, but after everything that's gone down lately, and seeing the hurt in his eyes, well, I just can't do it.

"Brian Miller is my former boss in California. He was never anything more than that. I need to call him—thanks for the reminder, by the way—because I forgot to empty the bottom drawer of my desk when I moved out of my office. There are some things in there I need. I'm hoping he'll have his admin send me the contents of said drawer."

Xander blinks, his shoulders drooping.

"Shit, I'm sorry."

"I'm not mad. And you're right. I *don't* owe you an explanation because we were not together. But for the love of Freya, X, I *did* just go through the most traumatic thing in my life back then. I was definitely *not* over you, and there was no way in hell I was looking to start something with anyone—even if it was just sex. Which there was none."

He swallows hard and nods, clearly fighting emotion.

"I know things are weird, and I don't know what's going to happen, but there's never been anyone else. *Never.* So, there's no need to be jealous or to get all worked up over some nerdy professor named Brian, who, although nice, thought that everything I taught was a bunch of woo-woo nonsense."

"Got it." He nods and meets my gaze. "Thanks for explaining."

"You're welcome. What are you up to today?"

"I have some business to see to, so I'll be doing paper-work. How about you?"

"Well, I've given my cousins enough space and time to give me the silent treatment. I'm going to get them together, apologize, say a bunch of words that will hope-fully help because I miss them, and then we can all get on with our lives."

"Good. You need to do that. For many reasons."

"I know." I finish my coffee and set the empty mug in the sink. Suddenly, Xander is behind me, wrapping his arms around my shoulders and hugging me to his rock-hard chest.

"I'm sorry," he says again. "And, for the record, there's never been anyone else for me, either."

"I know." I brace my hands on his arms but don't move to turn around and face him. There is nothing in the world like being in Xander's arms—never has been.

"I would have felt it if there had been someone. And so would *you*. So, there's nothing to wonder about."

"I know that, too," he says softly. "But when I saw the note, instinct kicked in. And I won't apologize for that."

"Understood."

He kisses my head, rests his lips in my hair, and breathes me in.

Goddess, I want him. If he asked me, here and now, to go to the bedroom and spend the day with him, I'd willingly go.

I can't resist him. I never could.

Maybe that's why my walls were so damn high for as long as they were when it came to this man. Because as soon as I lower them, even just a little, I'm a complete goner.

"Say hi to Breena and Lucy for me." He steps back, and I feel the loss of him all the way to my bones. "And would you do me a favor and just let me know when you get there? After the accident, I don't want to take any chances."

"No need," I inform him as I turn around and smile at him. "Breena's picking me up. They might be mad, but they're not taking any chances, either."

"Even better. I'll be at my house for the day. Jonas is going to join me there so we can do some reading and thinking together."

"Okay. I'll be in touch." Before I walk away, I quickly

hug him, pat his back, and then head for the door. "See you."

I hear him mutter, "Yes, you will."

"Thanks for the ride." I buckle my seat belt and then turn to look at my sweet cousin. "I love you. I need to say that first and foremost."

"You know I love you, too," she says and reaches over to take my hand as she pulls down my drive, headed toward Lucy's house. "Loving doesn't mean we don't get mad or hurt. Sometimes, I think when you love someone so much, that's when you get hurt and mad the most."

"You're probably right." With her hand still in mine, I watch Salem pass by. Now that we're firmly into October, even if it is early October, the townspeople have begun decorating their homes for Halloween, much to the delight of the tourists. "They'll close most of the streets downtown off to traffic in another week or so."

"Thursday," Breena confirms. "Walking traffic only. It's already almost too busy to drive through most of downtown now. Giles has been walking to work."

"I don't love that." I turn to look at her. "He's more vulnerable that way."

"There are so many people around when he's walking, it's unlikely *it* will go for him then."

I don't want to scare Breena, so I don't argue, but I

think *it* has balls and doesn't give a shit about having an audience.

I'll ask Xander what he thinks about Giles walking to work and get his take on it later.

Breena parks in front of the Blood Moon Apothecary, and we both hop out of the car and walk around the building to the gardens in the back. Lucy gave us a heads-up that we should meet outside, away from customers and listening ears.

We've always loved being outside together.

Lucy has already spread our quilt on the grass, the one we made together as kids, and she's in the middle of what looks to be harvesting sweet peas.

"I thought sweet peas were a spring flower," I say as we approach.

Lucy looks up and grins. "They usually are, but I can get some to bloom in the fall when it's cooler."

"And any other time," Breena adds with a knowing smile. "Lucy can make anything grow anywhere."

"It's my gift." Lucy shrugs and gestures for us to sit on the quilt. "I have some pumpkin spice lattes on the way for us. Jonas is fetching them."

"I love fall," Breena says with a happy sigh, closing her eyes and breathing in the crisp autumn air. "And the delicious drinks that come with it."

"You know, we can make pumpkin spice all year round," I remind her. "We don't have to save it for this time of year."

"I don't think it packs the same punch in July as it

does in October," Lucy says, turning her hurt, cool gaze on me. "Now, let's stop circling around the subject at hand."

"I love you," I say immediately, just how I did with Breena. "More than anything, I love you both, and I'm sorry I hurt you. If I could go back and change it all, I would in a heartbeat. Is there a tapestry we can weave to make that happen?"

Lucy deflates. "Just when I have a good mad going, you go and ruin it. No need to weave another magical tapestry. But we do need to talk this out. Because *Lorelei.*"

"I know."

We hear footsteps, and all of us turn to see Jonas walking toward us, so tall, lean, and handsome, carrying a tray filled with hot to-go cups.

"I have a delivery," he says with that kind smile of his as he squats and offers one to each of us.

"Did you get yourself one, too?" Lucy asks him, eyeing the fourth cup on the tray.

"No, I got one for Delia. She's earned it. Have a good chat, ladies."

He winks at his wife, and then he's off, headed into the apothecary.

"Jonas is pretty great," I say as I sip my drink. "And I agree with you. This just hits differently in October. So good. Anyway, back on topic."

We all sip our drinks happily.

"You were right, Luce. And, man, that pissed me off

at the time, but you're totally right. For whatever reason, I wanted to wear my hurt and anger like a shield against Xander, and I didn't call you guys to help me pretty much out of stubborn spite. It was wrong and childish."

"Why didn't you tell us *after*?" Breena asks. "That's what I don't understand. I can see you being scared and confused while it was all happening—and things can happen quickly. But after, you still didn't tell us anything."

"Because it was done, and you didn't know about the baby in the first place. I just thought I'd spare you all that hurt."

Lucy narrows her eyes at me.

"Don't call that out as bullshit. Even if it sounds like BS, it's not. That's really how I felt about it in the moment, whether it's right or wrong. And, yes, I can see now that it's wrong. I mean, I didn't even tell my *mom*. And I should have, because I could have used all your support, both then and now."

"Well, you have it now," Lucy says, rolling her eyes.

"I do? But you're so mad at me."

"Of course, I'm mad at you. But I love you. Even though you're a big jerk."

That makes me grin at her. "Yeah, I *am* a big jerk."

"The biggest," Breena agrees gleefully as she sips her delicious drink.

"I thought this would be so much harder," I admit and stare down at the lid of my latte. "Because you've never been that mad at me before, even when I acciden-tally cut your bangs too short in the sixth grade."

"I felt betrayed," Lucy admits softly. "I felt like the world had fallen out from under me. Because out of all the possible things you could have said happened, that was the last thing I would have expected. The three of us tell each other everything. *Everything*. And you were going to have a baby and didn't tell us."

"I wanted it to be an awesome Yule surprise. There were so many moments that I wanted to tell you. I almost just blurted it out several times. But I didn't find out until I was about ten weeks along. My periods have always been wonky, so I didn't think much of it, and then Xander suggested I take a test just to be sure. And there it was. So, I saw the doctor, and it was so close to Yule we decided to wait."

"It would have been a lovely Yule gift," Breena assures me, always the peacekeeper. "And we would have loved it."

"Thank you." I lean over and bump her shoulder with mine. "I'm not proud of any of it. And I can say that I went to California to get away from Xander, but the truth is, I ran away so I could avoid all of it. So I wouldn't have to tell you about it, and I wouldn't have to think about the baby or look at Xander and feel resent-ment and vulnerability with him."

"You've never been good at being vulnerable," Lucy points out.

"No. I'm not good at it at all, and I don't like it. So,

of course, I ran away from it. And, added to that, I needed to heal. Physically, I was a mess."

"Of course, you were," Breena says. "Your body went through a huge trauma."

"Yeah, and I had depression and some PTSD. I got some therapy in California in addition to all the classes I took. I think I had to find myself again and figure out some stuff before I could come home and be any good to anyone else."

"Don't do that again," Lucy says sternly. "If some big shit goes down, we help each other."

"I won't. Goddess willing, it won't happen again, but I'll never shut you two out. I can promise you that."

"Good." Lucy nods, sipping her drink.

"Now, I need your help."

They both look at me in surprise, and I can't help but laugh.

"Yes, I know, I'm asking for help. But damn it, I need some advice."

"I'm all ears," Breena says. "What's up?"

I fill them in on Xander living with me and watch as their faces change from interest, to surprise, to smugness.

"So, he's living with you," Lucy says thoughtfully. "How...convenient."

"He's not sleeping with me."

"Lorelei, you didn't make him sleep on that horrible, tiny twin bed, did you?" Breena says, horrified.

"I was going to, but then I took pity on him. He's in my bed, and I'm on the twin."

"And what do you need help with?" Lucy asks.

"You guys." I set my cup aside and rub my hands over my face in agitation. "I don't know what's happened, but my walls with Xander are slipping, *crumbling*, and I'll be damned if I'm not...catching feelings."

"What kind of feelings?" Breena wants to know.

I eye her speculatively. "You're going to make me spell it out, aren't you?"

"Well, you're the only mind reader here. So, yes," Lucy chimes in. "What kind of feelings are you catching, Lora?"

"The fuzzy, sexy, jump-your-bones and climb-you-like-a-tree but also red-cartoon-hearts-exploding-over-my-head feelings."

I bury my face in my hands. When they don't say anything for a long five seconds, I peek out from between my fingers to find them both grinning at me.

"What?"

"You're meant," Breena says simply.

"But—"

"No buts," Lucy interrupts. "It is what it is. You could fight it. You could go back to California or go to Zimbabwe, but it won't change what is. You and Xander are soulmates in the most real sense of the word. It would make sense that your heart would open back up to him as you heal."

"He thinks we should give it another try. And when I said it was bad timing, he disagreed. Said our bond is stronger when we're together."

"Absolutely," Breena agrees, nodding her head. "There are few bonds stronger than that between two fated people. It absolutely makes you more powerful and a force to be reckoned with."

"I don't have time for romance," I object. "I need to help lift a curse and kill the bad guy. There's no time for dates and stolen kisses."

"There's always time for stolen kisses," Lucy points out. "And if you're stopping at kisses, you're not taking full advantage of that hot man. Lorelei, he's *gorgeous*. If I weren't so in love with my husband, and if you weren't tethered to him, and, well, a million other reasons, I'd cast a love spell on Xander myself."

"Ditto," Breena agrees. "And I was bitter for a long time that he doesn't have a brother. An identical *twin* brother."

I can't help but laugh, relieved that all the tension from the hurt I caused them is gone.

"He really is the very definition of sexy." I worry my lower lip between my teeth. "You guys, I admit that I haven't had sex with anyone but Xander—"

"Like, *ever*?" Lucy blinks rapidly. "With *no one* else?"

"Wow," Breena breathes.

"I was always meant for him," I remind them. "Anyway, I know he's the only one I've been with, so I don't exactly have a yardstick to measure against, but the sex with Xander is *insane*. Like, I'm shocked the earth doesn't shake, the heavens don't weep, and the oceans don't heave. Wait, the oceans *do* heave. We've had sex on the water a lot."

"Define a lot," Breena says, leaning closer.

"He used to take me out on his boat at least a few times a week. You get a sea witch and a crazy powerful eclectic witch having sex on the water, and well...it's wild."

"I'm so jealous right now," Lucy murmurs, and I laugh.

"So, what, exactly, do you need advice on?" Breena asks. "Because it sounds like you know exactly what you want. You want to bang the hell out of Xander."

"I really do." I nod dreamily. "But we have a history, and if I get hurt again, I don't think I'll survive it."

"You do have a history, and the hurt was half your fault." I stare at Lucy, but she just shakes her head. "You know it was, Lora, you stubborn witch. He's under your roof for the foreseeable future. You love each other. You're definitely hot for each other."

"So hot," I murmur.

"Do it," Breena says, clapping her hands. "Just do it already. Stop making excuses, stop dwelling, use the power you found while you were away, and do what makes you happy, honey. If we've learned anything over the past few years, it's that life can be way too short. If he makes you happy and makes your heart sing—"

"And your lady bits tingle," Lucy adds with a grin.

"—then be with Xander. Love him. Let him love you back. Talk about your hurts and move on from them.

Don't hold them against him anymore. Don't bring up the past in current arguments just to hurt each other. Because that's not fair."

"Are you a shrink now?" I ask, but I know she's right. They're both right.

"I'm smart, and I know you. I know you both. You belong together."

"We could start singing old Mariah Carey songs," Lucy suggests, but I just laugh and shake my head.

"I'm so glad I came over here and that we straightened everything out. *And* I got some good advice."

"We always give good advice," Lucy says. "I know it's hard to open yourself up when you're afraid of being hurt. But, honey, it could be the best thing you ever do. It could be *wonderful*. Don't miss out on wonderful just because you're afraid of a few bruises."

"I can handle the bruises; it's the knife to my heart I'm afraid of."

"Not gonna happen." Breena sounds so sure. "I'm psychic enough to know that much."

"Thank you. Oh, Breena, Xander said we need to go check on your house. He thinks there might be a water leak inside."

"Damn it," she mutters with a scowl.

Breena hasn't lived in her little house since the night *it* tried to kill her almost a year ago. She just couldn't go back there, and I don't blame her. But since that night, the paranormal activity has been too crazy for her to sell it to some unsuspecting buyer.

We need to do a deep clean on that place, both spiritually and physically, but we haven't had the time.

"We could go over there now," Lucy suggests. "Jonas will go with us."

"I'll call Giles. If I go there without him, he'll spike my morning coffee with rat poison."

"That's very specific." I laugh and reach for my phone. "I'll tell Xander. We might as well all go together."

"It's better if we're together," Breena agrees.

"Am I the only one who doesn't want to go in there?" I ask as we all stand in the driveway, staring at the small house.

Somehow, in the past few months, it's been reclaimed by ivy and weeds and looks like it's been abandoned for decades rather than less than a year.

And that doesn't even begin to describe the activity.

"Is that a...goat on the roof?" Giles asks. "With human eyes?"

"For the love of Poseidon, this is creepy as hell," I say. "I would reach out with my mind to see inside, but I don't think it's safe."

"You will *not*," Xander says, his voice hard, and his eyes full of fire. "No one is going in yet. We have some work to do first. Please, tell me you're all shielded."

"Crystals, oils, spells, you name it," I assure him.

"All of us," Jonas confirms.

"Good."

Xander lifts his arms, and the wind picks up immediately. Instinctively, I know which spell he's going to do, and so do the others. We begin chanting at the same time.

"Sage and crystals, salt and wood, purify this house, leave only good. Gods and goddesses, guardians, guides, root out the evil where it likes to hide. Banish the taint, cleanse the space, this is our will, purify this place!"

The wind is brutal, whipping us mercilessly. Finally, there's a scream from inside the house, the inhuman one we've heard several times now, and then everything goes perfectly calm.

"We only have minutes," Giles says. "Because it'll come right back."

"Agreed," Xander says, already eating up the ground with his long strides. He pushes the door open, and water comes gushing out at us, soaking our feet. "Get out of the water!"

We all back out of the flow, careful not to let it touch us. Water conducts paranormal activity, and we don't need it sticking to any of us.

"Where is it coming from?" Breena asks.

"I'm looking," I inform her, closing my eyes. Goddess, the inside of the house is completely unrecognizable. I'm so glad Breena can't go in.

This would tear her heart apart. She loved this house.

"I don't see any leaks," I say at last, even after looking everywhere.

"I don't either," Xander confirms.

"Could it be coming up from the ground?" Jonas wants to know. "Through the floor?"

"Groundwater," I murmur thoughtfully. "I need to tap into my element to look."

"You'll be damn careful," Xander says. I can tell his nerves are stretched thin.

I know he wants me—and the rest of us—out of here.

"Of course, I will."

I back up even farther and lift my hands, then take a deep breath and call on water. My voice is loud and strong in my head as I pull in the strength of my element to amplify my power.

When I dip down under the surface of the earth, searching, I'm knocked back on my ass, pulling me out of my trance.

"Ouch."

The others are around me immediately, helping me to my feet.

"What did you see?" Breena asks.

My gaze turns to Xander, and I nod. "It's coming from the ground."

CHAPTER NINE
XANDER

"Why the groundwater?" Giles asks, leaning back in his chair across from me as he takes his dark-rimmed glasses off and rubs at his eyes. "And why Breena's house?"

"He's used the house in the past," Jonas points out. "It's like he's drawing energy from it or something."

"True, and I can tell you that when we had to go there to get her loom last spring, it was full of activity."

"It has been all year," I add. "And each time we've gone, it's only been more active each time."

"It's why Breena avoids it," Giles murmurs and stands to pace behind the table in my library. The three of us came straight here to do some reading and brainstorming while the girls went to Lucy's to cook up some *witchy stuff*, as Lorelei put it.

As long as she's not alone, I'm okay.

"Don't get me wrong," Giles continues, rubbing his

neck. He's hurting physically, so I narrow my eyes and scan him to see if I can tell what's wrong.

Aside from the stress we currently have going on, that is.

"She avoids the house primarily because of the memory of what happened to her there last year, and I don't think anyone can blame her for that."

"Absolutely not," Jonas agrees, also narrowing his eyes on the other man. He glances over at me, and I give him a slight nod.

I see it, too.

"But also, the activity happening in the house keeps her away," Giles continues, still rubbing at his neck. "And now it's all flooded, and I could see from the look on her face that she's devastated. She still had things in there she thought she could save later, although I don't know that she'd ever want to bring any of it home. But the hope was there."

He twitches as if he has an itch in his back.

"Are you feeling all right, Giles?" I ask calmly.

"Huh?" He glances at me and then nods. "Oh, yeah, I'm fine. Just antsy, I guess."

"Can I look you over?" Jonas asks, his voice just as calm and steady as mine. "I can heal you, you know."

"No. No, I'm just fine. Anyway, the water is so weird. Breena had the main water line shut off." He kicks out a leg as if it's fallen asleep and has gone numb.

"Lorelei figured out it's coming through the ground," I remind him, watching as he scowls.

"Who? Oh, Lorelei. Right. That's right. But if it's the groundwater that's rising, how can it get into the house?"

"There's likely a crawlspace under the floor or something. It's probably coming up that way," Jonas says, watching Giles just as closely as I am. "Are you sure I can't help?"

"I said no. Now, fuck off," Giles growls, wiping the back of his hand over his mouth.

Immediately, Jonas and I look at each other and begin the spell.

"Elements of sun, Fire and Earth of day, lend us your strength to cast evil away. Elements of night, Water and Air of moon, lend us your might and make it soon. Magick of one, power of all, protect this witch, heed our call."

Giles bends forward at the waist, and then the wind picks up, swirling around us. I wave my hand to the window, opening it, and the energy flies out of the house. With another flick of the wrist, the window closes, and I know it's gone.

"What in the actual fuck?" Giles asks, breathing hard, his face breaking out in a sweat.

"Something attached itself to you at the house and took a little ride," I reply, still looking closely. "How do you feel?"

"Pissed the hell off."

"Can I have a look now?" Jonas asks, standing to cross the room to him.

"Please. Have all the looks you need."

Jonas lays his hand on Giles's forehead, closes his eyes, and takes a long, deep breath.

"It's gone," he says after a few moments. "Only Giles. And I happen to prefer that."

"I think we all do." Still watching Giles, I stand to pour some water into a glass and pass it to my friend. "Here, drink this."

"Gladly." He takes a deep drink and seems to calm some, retaking his seat at the table. "That was as weird as it gets. I was perfectly fine, and then I just...wasn't here. It was like I was in the background, watching."

"Was it painful?" Jonas inquires.

"No, just damn weird. I hope the girls are okay."

Immediately, I reach for my phone and call Lorelei.

"You just interrupted a spell," she says upon answering. "What's up?"

I quickly explain what just happened to Giles. "Are the three of you okay?"

"Poor Giles," she says with a sigh. "Yeah, we all seem fine. If anything changes, I'll let you know."

"Do that. Keep an eye out."

"Will do. I have to tell the girls. Kiss Giles for me."

"I absolutely will not do that."

She's laughing as she disconnects.

"They're safe?" Giles asks.

"Yes," Jonas replies. "I just spoke with Lucy telepathically."

"Lorelei also says they're fine."

"Good." Giles rubs his forehead, but it's a completely different movement from before. More...*Giles.* "Okay, let's keep going."

"Do you want to rest?" Jonas asks him.

"No, I want to figure this shit out. I'm really okay. A little tired, but mostly just unnerved, you know?"

"Yeah." I nod at my best friend. "I know. Okay, moving on. If *it* is in the groundwater, he can get anywhere in Salem."

"We don't know that he's *in* the water," Jonas replies thoughtfully. "But I agree with you that, at the very least, he's using the water for energy."

"Makes sense," Giles says, thinking it over. "When we defeated it at Beltane, you were in the water, Xander. It dispersed into the water."

"I hadn't thought of that," I murmur. "You're absolutely right. I wonder if that's why Lorelei hears music coming from the harbor and bay."

"What?" Jonas demands, his voice sharper than I've ever heard it before.

"I've been meaning to ask you both about this. I didn't want to bring it up when Lorelei was with us because I don't want to scare her. Several times now, I've found her standing near the shoreline, in some sort of trance. She just stares out at the water and doesn't respond when I talk to her. It's not until I touch her that she snaps out of it. And every single time, she asks me if I can hear the music. She *loves* the music, but then she feels sick until we're back inside the house."

"Godsdamn it, it's fucking with her." Giles makes a fist and thumps it against my table. "It's doing the siren thing."

"I agree," Jonas says, nodding. "Giles, didn't you once make a comment that Lorelei believes in mermaids and other sea creatures?"

"She believes in all of it," I reply before Giles can. "She used to swear that she saw the merpeople."

"I've never seen anyone so in tune with their element the way Lorelei is," Jonas continues. "Even my mother, who was also a sea witch, wasn't as gifted as Lorelei, and she was extremely powerful."

"Wait." I hold up my hand and the grimoire I need floats off the shelf and into my grasp. "This is your sister's Book of Shadows. Maybe she made some notes about your mother's gifts."

"I still can't believe you have Jonas's sister's grimoire," Giles says, shaking his head. "How did it survive more than three hundred years?"

"Witches are sentimental," I reply with a shrug. "Ancestors are a big deal. The witches in my family didn't throw anything away, and while that used to annoy me, I'm damn grateful now."

"As am I," Jonas replies softly, staring at the book before me. "It was a nice surprise the day you showed me Katrina's book. She was diligent in keeping notes and writing everything down."

"You were close to her."

He looks up at me and offers me a small smile. "I

loved both my sisters, but I was closest to Katrina. She was older than me by a few years and was my constant friend. We enjoyed writing spells together. In fact, she helped me write the curse of the blood moon."

"She helped you but didn't write anything about it in her grimoire?" Giles asks.

"Even if she'd written it down, it would have disappeared when I cast the curse," Jonas replies easily. "She likely did record it. When it disappeared, she wrote over the pages."

"You were too thorough with that curse, man." Giles frowns at the book in front of me.

"It was life and death. There was no room for error."

I gingerly flip through the pages, not wanting to rip or ruin the fragile paper. "There are plenty of water spells here, and she makes reference to some of them being from a...Marjorie."

"That's my mother," Jonas says, leaning forward.

"Katrina recorded everything, but she didn't use this book as a diary. However, we may be able to find a spell in here to help us with our current water situation."

"That would be helpful," Giles says, blowing out a breath. "Does it say anything about siren songs?"

"It's a big book." I look over at Giles. "It looks like Katrina had just the one grimoire for her entire life, and it's damn big."

"Looks like you have some homework," Giles replies with a grin.

"We all do." Jonas taps the table. "My friend, Louisa,

may be stuck on a time loop in 1692, but that doesn't mean she doesn't have knowledge about these things. I'll ask her about water spells when I go back to Hallows End tomorrow morning."

"I forget we can use your coven for information," I admit. "If she has any advice, we'd love to hear it."

"I'll find out what I can without giving her any specifics."

"I'm going to talk to my parents," Giles adds. "They'll know, or at least have knowledge about, where to find some things. We need to start utilizing our coven if we're going to resolve all of this in less than a month."

"You're right. And I know everyone wants to help. I just hoped to keep them out of harm's way."

"We need them," Giles counters. "And if they're willing to help, I say we use them."

"I'll call a coven meeting."

"I'd like to go get my girl." Giles stands from the table. "Make sure she's safe."

"I think we should all do that," Jonas replies, also standing. "It'll calm our nerves."

"Hell, yes." I close the book and tuck it under my arm as I join the others. "I'll do my homework later."

"**W**ait."

Lorelei turns and plants her hand on my chest, stopping me from climbing her front porch steps. My hands are loaded down with grocery bags.

"This stuff is gonna melt."

Her lips twitch. "Before we go in, I want to set a rule for tonight."

"You don't usually set rules."

"I am right now. No more talk of what happened today, *it*, or the curse for the rest of the evening. I just want a few hours of peace."

"Done. Can I go set these down now?"

"Yes." She turns and unlocks the door, then steps inside. I follow her. "You always loved junk food just a little too much."

She pulls a bag of nacho cheese tortilla chips out of a grocery bag and stows it in the pantry.

"We all have our faults."

"I'm going to make fish tacos for dinner. What do you think?"

"Sounds great to me. Good thing I got regular tortilla chips, too. And salsa."

"I can make guac, as well. And it's not even Taco Tuesday."

"It can be Taco Friday." I wink at her and finish putting the groceries away while she pulls out a cutting board and gets started on the guacamole. "So, what *do* you want to talk about since everything else is off the table?"

"I don't know." She slices into a tomato. "I guess there's nothing else to talk about, is there?"

"Not true. How did it go with the girls today? You all seemed fine by the time we saw you."

"It went well. Thank the goddess." She drops the tomato chunks into a bowl and reaches for an onion. "My mom's birthday is coming up. I wonder what I should get her. She already has just about everything."

"I can't help with that." I laugh and kiss her cheek, then walk around the peninsula and sit on a stool while she continues to chop. "Speaking of moms, mine and Grandma are coming up next week."

That makes her pause in surprise. "From Florida?"

"Yep. They want to be here through Samhain."

"But, Xander, it's so dangerous right now."

"I know, and I tried to tell them that, but you know how stubborn they are. They want to be here. They think they can help."

"Well, everyone will be thrilled to see them. They left a big hole in the coven when they left. I know the warmer climate is better for your grandmother, but they've been missed."

"I know." My gods, I want to touch her. Being with her to protect her is the right thing to do, but she'd tempt a saint, and I've never claimed that title. I want her with every ounce of my being.

And it saddens me to know that we may never get to a place where she'll allow me to touch her like that again.

With the guacamole finished and in the fridge, Lorelei heats up a pan and pours in a little oil for the fish.

I've discovered that I love to watch her cook. Back in the day, she could burn salad. Now, she easily whips up meals so delicious it always surprises me.

"Why are you smiling at me like that?"

I don't drop the smile. "Because you're sexy in the kitchen."

She rolls her eyes, but I see the flush of amusement and pleasure filling her cheeks. Lora never could take a compliment well, but I could always tell she enjoyed receiving them.

And I never had a problem giving them.

Because every single complimentary word was absolutely true—still is.

"Maybe I should just wear my little black apron and nothing else."

"If you do that, the little bit of self-control I have left will snap."

She blinks as if surprised.

"Do you think I don't want you?"

"No, I—" She swallows hard and then simply turns to me. "I don't know what to say to that."

"I always did appreciate your honesty. I want you so badly that I ache with it, Lorelei. Always have. Always will. Absolutely nothing will change that."

She bites her lip.

"So, if you don't mind if my control takes a vacation, then...by all means. Wear the apron."

To my surprise, she doesn't put the fish in the skillet. Instead, she turns off the burner, stows the food in the fridge, and then marches out of the room, leaving me to curse myself.

I'm a complete idiot.

I just ruined the small foothold of trust and ease we'd gained and started to rebuild between us, and all because I want to get her naked.

Just as I'm about to get up and follow her, to apologize and reassure her, she comes marching back into the kitchen, naked as the day she was born, aside from that little black apron.

My tongue is glued to the roof of my mouth as I take her in. Her dark auburn hair is long and curly, draped around her shoulders. Her eyes, as green as a stormy ocean, are on fire as she watches my gaze move from the top of her head to the tips of her little pink toes.

"Wow."

"My cousins gave me some good advice today."

"Yeah?" I can't stop staring at the smooth skin of her shoulders. "What's that?"

"They said I should grab hold of what I want and what makes me happy because life can be so short."

"Good advice." I have to swallow hard. "Excellent advice. And what do you want, Lorelei? What makes you happy?"

My fingers twitch. I want to reach for her, so I ball my hands into fists, staring at her.

"You." She flips her hair over her shoulder, standing proud and sure. "Being with you makes me happy, Xander."

"I hope this means you're okay with me putting my hands on you."

She holds her arms out at her sides. "I'm all yours."

"Thank fuck."

I move in, but I remind myself to be gentle. I'm strong, and I don't want to hurt her. I twirl a piece of that fiery hair around my finger and lean in to press my lips to hers as I reach behind her with my other hand and pull the ties of the apron free.

It takes less than a second to pull the loop over her head and toss the whole thing to the floor, and then, I simply scoop her up into my arms and march back to the bedroom.

"I thought we might have kitchen sex," she murmurs against my neck.

"That's on my list for later. First, I want you in a bed because I plan to take my time. It's been a damn long time, baby."

"That's my fault."

I cut off that thought by kissing her senseless and then set her gently on the bed. "We're not talking about fault or hurt or any of the rest of it. Because that's over, Lorelei. It's in the past, and we can't change it. We're going to move forward from here, and I'm going to just love the fuck out of you."

"I'm down for that. But first, you have to get naked."

Ignoring her, I kiss my way down her chest and nuzzle her nipple with my nose before sucking it into my mouth. Her hands dive into my hair, holding on tightly as her legs scissor in anticipation.

She's so damn *responsive.* Enthusiastic.

Gorgeous.

My hands can't get their fill as they roam over her smooth, amazing curves. And when they drift up her inner thigh, she gasps and grabs for my shirt.

"Get. Naked. Xander. You're not allowed to touch me there until your clothes are off, damn it."

"Yes, ma'am." Lorelei calls the shots, always. So, I immediately stand, make quick work of my black shirt and jeans, and then join her once more. "Now, where was I?"

She willingly spreads her legs, so ready for me to explore and tease, to coax and pleasure her. She leaves wet kisses on my shoulder, my chest.

And, finally, my fingers make it to her already wet and ready center.

She grips onto me, her eyes wide and on mine as if she's almost scared of what's about to happen.

"What's wrong?" I kiss her chin and then her nose and wait to move closer to her folds. "Talk to me, baby."

"I'm not the same."

My eyes narrow on hers, and I can see the fear there.

"I'm not the same as I used to be. I have scars, and I don't know if it'll feel the same."

She closes her eyes, clearly embarrassed. "Hey. Look at me."

She just bites her lip, but she still doesn't open her eyes.

"Lorelei, heart of my heart, open your beautiful eyes."

Reluctantly, she does, and I see they're shining with unshed tears.

"We're not going to do anything you're not ready for. You know that. You're the boss. Always."

"You always said that." She drags her hand down my cheek. "I guess I'm just nervous."

"Me, too."

Her eyebrows climb. "You're not nervous."

"Are you kidding? We haven't done this in a really long time, and there's a whole lot of baggage between us since that last time. It's a lot of pressure."

"Okay, we make a deal."

"Another rule?"

"If you like. Let's toss the baggage. It's heavy."

"Too heavy."

"And I'll try to not be filled with paralyzing fear that you won't like the way my body is now."

"Have you not seen my face every time I look at you?"

She just smirks. "And you'll toss the pressure out with the baggage. It's just us. Today. Right now."

"Just us." I can't hold back from kissing her again, and she clings to me as she gives as good as she gets. "You okay?"

"Yeah." She takes a deep breath. "Yeah, my freak-out moment is over."

"If you have any more of those, it's all right. Got it?"

She nods, but rather than going back to where I was, I start from the very beginning.

And feel her relax against me.

CHAPTER TEN
LORELEI

I always used to think that Xander put some kind of a spell on me while we had sex. He puts me in this happy, floaty, burning haze every time we're together like this, but I know now that it's not a sex spell.

It's just the chemistry between us.

The bond between my soul and Xander's is so strong that whenever we make love, it's as though we've been doing it for centuries.

And, if I believe what he's always said, we've done exactly that—through many lifetimes.

"You don't have to go that slow." I grin when he lifts his head from where he's making sure my chest gets plenty of attention and narrows his eyes at me. "I'm not complaining. I'm just saying I'm okay now."

"Good. I'm great, too."

And with that, he goes back to licking the underside

of my breast, making me squirm. It's one of my most sensitive spots, and he clearly remembers that all too well.

"Xander." I can't help but writhe under him, wishing he'd move much, much lower.

"Hmm?"

"I'm gonna need...oh, shit." Was it just moments ago that I was all self-conscious and worried? Because now all I can think about is getting him inside me.

ASAP.

"What do you need?" He nibbles his way around my navel.

"You." I swallow and just about come off the bed when he bites my flesh, just below my belly button. "In me. Now."

"Look at me."

I peel my eyes open and look down to where he's settled between my legs, enjoying me.

"Are you sure?"

"Don't I sound sure?"

He grins and then hovers over me, braced on one arm, as he guides himself to me. He's *right there*, but he doesn't push in.

"Xander."

"I love you," he says, those dark eyes pinned to mine. "I wanted to go ahead and get that out because it's really cliché to say it during."

My blood warms how it always does when he says those words to me. I cup his cheeks in my hands.

"I love you, too. Now, please, if you don't fuck me, I'm going to lose my shit here."

He smirks, and then he oh so slowly fills me. It takes me a moment to adjust to him because it *has* been a while, and he's a big guy.

But then he begins to move, and I anchor my legs up high on his hips. It's as though something in the universe just clicks into place.

Like I've come home.

I have to close my eyes to hide the tears that want to fall. If he sees them, he'll stop, fearing he's hurt me.

When, in reality, I was the one hurting myself all along.

He pushes me up, and when I'm at the precipice of falling into bliss, Xander plants his lips near my ear and whispers, "Go, baby. Go over for me."

How can I resist that strong, rough command?

I can't.

I fall, clinging to him as wave after wave of glorious sensation rolls through me. He thrusts twice and then follows me.

"It's windy in here," I realize as I gaze around the room and see the curtains billowing and papers moving.

The window isn't open.

"We've always been powerful," Xander replies as he rolls to the side to take his weight off me. "Did you hear the thunder?"

"There wasn't thunder."

A self-satisfied grin spreads over his ridiculously handsome face. "Oh, yeah. There was thunder."

"You look awfully pleased with yourself."

"I don't think there's been a moment in my life when I was *more* pleased than I am right now." He tips my chin up so he can kiss me softly. "Are you okay?"

"I think I rank at least a few notches above okay. I'm bordering on fantastic."

"Good."

"Are you hungry?"

"Starving."

I smirk and climb out of bed, walking into the closet to fetch a robe. "Me, too. I'll go make the tacos. It'll only take a minute since everything is pretty much already prepped."

After making a stop in the restroom, I pad into the kitchen and start the burner to heat up the skillet once more, humming under my breath.

My girls were right today. Going after what I want, following my damn heart, feels better than I thought it would. I'm relieved to let the past go and allow myself to feel the love and desire for Xander that I've kept locked away for so long.

And all of it because of my own stubbornness.

With the fish cooking, I gather the rest of the supplies from the fridge and pantry. When I turn back toward the room, I jump at the sight of Xander filling the doorway.

"Sorry," he says, holding up his hands. "I thought you heard me stomping down the hallway."

"For a man your size, you don't make much noise when you walk. It's fascinating. This will be ready in about five minutes."

"What's your favorite thing to cook?" he asks as I get to work assembling the tacos. He tried to help me cook on the first night, but he just gets in my way, so he agreed to be a spectator.

"I actually don't love to cook."

"Oh, you don't have—"

"I know I don't have to." I shake my head. "I don't mind it. I know I'm good at it. It's baking that I really love. The more challenging, the better. I keep meaning to get Aunt Hilda's sourdough starter from her. I've been in the mood to bake some bread."

"Do you know how to make brownies?"

I raise an eyebrow as I pass his plate to him.

"Of course, I do."

"Well, if you ever want to make a pan of brownies and share them, I wouldn't complain."

"I'll remember that."

Dinner is nice. Actually, the whole evening has just been really *nice*. It almost feels like the old days, before the baby, when we were just young and so in love we couldn't see straight.

Finally, when I can't hold my eyes open for another minute, I yawn. "I think I have to go to bed. I'm exhausted, and I want to get an early start to the day tomorrow. I need to get some writing in."

"I think we both could use some rest."

We work together to make sure the house is locked up and the lights are off, before making our way down the hall. When I reach for the knob of the guest room door, Xander stops me.

"What are you doing?"

"I'm going to bed."

"That's not your room."

I frown at the guest room door and then look up at Xander. "Do you think I'm going to sleep with you just because I had sex with you?"

"That's exactly what I *know.*"

I grin. "Okay. I have to go wash my face."

I breeze past him and through my bedroom to the bathroom. I figured I'd be sleeping with Xander tonight —and likely every night—but I didn't want to be presumptuous.

And, I could admit, I wanted to see what his reaction would be.

He didn't disappoint.

With the water running in the sink, I wet my face, reach for my cleanser, and start scrubbing my cheeks, forehead, and nose. Then, I splash the warm water to rinse off the soap and reach for a towel to pat it somewhat dry.

Before I grab my moisturizer, I glance down into the basin of water and feel my heart stop.

The reflection isn't me.

Well, *technically*, it's me. But I look decomposed, half my skin gone, exposing teeth and gums. One eye is missing. My hair is stringy and thin.

"You hold no power here," I say, not giving in to the fear that wants to lick up my back and enter my heart. "Your tricks fall on deaf ears. In the light of day, in the darkness of night, I banish you from my sight."

The room hums with my energy. There's a whoosh of air, and the apparition is gone.

It can't get to me in my home. It can play tricks like that one, but it can't harm me or Xander. I have too many wards and too many protections set against it.

But damn if it isn't unnerving.

"Lorelei?"

"I'm fine," I call back and squirt some moisturizer into my palm, then walk out of the bathroom as I rub it into my face. "*It* tried to dick with me, but I sent it on its merry way. What does it say about me that it doesn't even really scare me all that much anymore? It's just annoying now."

I stop short when I see Xander standing in the middle of my bedroom, holding my pillow in one hand, and in the other...

"Oh."

"You still have this."

It's not a question as his gaze falls to the blanket he holds in his hand.

"I would have fetched my own pillow."

"I didn't mind." He swallows hard. "I know how picky you are about the pillows. I wasn't expecting to find this under it."

Feeling a little foolish and a *lot* exposed, I cross to him and take my pillow from him, tossing it onto the bed.

"I couldn't get rid of it."

As soon as we found out I was pregnant, we both knew the baby would be a girl. The first thing Xander did was run out and buy the softest, pinkest blanket he could find, bringing it home for the baby.

"I donated everything else," I continue when he doesn't reply. "But I just couldn't part with this. It reminded me of you and her, and I just needed that comfort."

"So, you sleep with it?"

"Yes." I raise my chin in defiance. "And I refuse to be embarrassed about that. Or apologize for it."

"I think it's pretty sweet," he murmurs. "Where do you want me to put it?"

I take it from him, fold it, and set it under my pillow as I always do.

"I keep it there."

"Okay. Now, did you say that *it* just tried to fuck with you?"

"Yeah. But don't worry. I pissed it off and sent it packing."

"That's my girl."

The words are flowing for the first time since Xander moved into my little waterfront cottage.

On top of having a killer to stop and a curse to lift, I'm on deadline.

I couldn't believe it when I sold my idea of a novel about folklore and legends surrounding the Salem area last year, and I *really* couldn't believe what the publisher was willing to pay for it.

I guess all that manifestation really paid off.

But now I have to write the book. They've already given me one extension, and I refuse to ask for another.

I've been hard at it since before the sun came up this morning. Xander popped his head in twice, once to bring me fresh coffee and then again to kiss me goodbye before leaving to meet up with Giles at our friend's gem and crystal shop downtown.

I love writing in the quiet. I have the window cracked so I can hear the waves, which also fills me with creativity and soothes me at the same time.

When I take a break for lunch, I plan to take a walk along the shoreline. I've avoided it lately because I just feel so damn *nauseous* when I'm near the water, but I really need to give it a try. I'm a sea witch. What good am I if I can't walk along the damn shore?

So, with a long walk as my motivation to finish the chapter I'm currently working on, I put my head down and let my fingers fly over the keyboard. It's rare that the story flows so freely, so I lean in to it and take full advantage.

More than an hour later, I sit back and roll my shoulders to work out the kinks as I read what I just wrote.

"Not bad," I murmur, then stand and reach high above my head. "If I keep this pace, I'll make the deadline with a few days to spare. That would be ideal and keep me in my editor's good graces."

Which is good because I'd really like to write another book when this one is finished.

It's been rainy all day today, so I pull on my yellow galoshes. I don't worry about a raincoat because the water doesn't really bother me. I just hate getting my feet wet unless it's on my own terms.

Armed with my basket for gathering treasures, and my phone tucked safely into my back pocket, I set off down the shoreline.

Taking a deep breath, I tip my head back and soak in the wet air and the scent of the ocean. Feeling confident with no nausea in sight, I walk farther away from home.

"Maybe it was just some kind of weird vertigo," I mutter to myself. "An inner ear infection or something silly like that."

I catch sight of an old, green glass bottle that has washed up on shore and snatch it up, setting it in my basket. As I glance at the sky, I see Xander flying overhead, croaking down at me. I offer him a smile and a wave.

I see that he's circling back toward the cottage, so I turn back and begin walking that way.

Before I've stepped five paces, I start to hear the music.

It's so loud and clear and so freaking beautiful. I don't know who is making music down at the pier, but they're very talented.

I'll have to ask around and find out who it is.

I stop walking and face the water, forgetting all about my basket and Xander, just watching the waves roll in as I listen to the music.

Like each time I hear it, my mind just lets go. I don't feel any stress—no worry at all, actually. It's such a wonderful break from the very real stressors I live with all the time now that I happily give in and let my shoulders fall, listening raptly.

I think there are lyrics. Maybe. I can't hear them clearly, but it sounds like a voice singing something along with the gorgeous music.

Someone touches my shoulder, and I turn to find Xander frowning down at me.

"I'm sorry, what?"

"You didn't hear me?"

"No. Were you calling for me?"

"I was yelling as loudly as I could from the house, then all the way down the shoreline as I made my way to you. You couldn't have *not* heard me."

"How weird." The nausea sets in again, and I have to

clamp my hand over my mouth. "Ugh, I don't feel so hot."

"Come on." His face is set in grim lines as he takes the basket from me, holds his other hand out for mine, then begins leading me back to the cottage. "We need to talk about this, Lorelei."

"Talk about what? The nausea? I was thinking it's probably some kind of weird vertigo or something. Did you hear the music?" I'm sad it's gone. "It's so pretty. I wish I knew who's playing it. They're so talented."

"That's what we need to talk about."

"What?"

"The music. You're the only one who can hear it, baby."

I scoff at that and shake my head. "No, you're just flying too high to hear it. I have to hurry back."

I pick up the pace, practically running back to the cottage. When I finally reach the door, I fling it open and rush for the bathroom.

This time, I lose my breakfast.

Thank the goddess I was able to make it to the toilet.

I can feel Xander lay a cold, wet rag on my neck after he picks up my hair and holds it away from my face.

This is like déjà vu. He did this for me all the time when I had morning sickness.

"Sorry," I mutter, then reach back to grab the washcloth, using it to wipe my mouth. "That's so gross."

"I'm just sorry it's happening to you."

Xander stands behind me at the sink as if I might fall

over at any minute, waiting while I rinse my mouth, brush my teeth, and then rinse again.

With the nausea passing, I turn and step into Xander's arms, hugging him tightly around his torso.

"How do you feel now?"

"Better. It's only ever bad when I'm out near the water. Today was the worst. I need to be by the water, Xander. I'm a freaking sea witch."

"I know." He kisses the top of my head. "I know you are. We'll figure this out."

"Maybe I should go to the doctor."

"I don't think it's medical, but you could have Jonas take a peek."

I frown at him as we walk down the hall to the living room, where I collapse onto the couch. "If it's not medical, then what is it? Because it feels pretty medical to me."

"I think *it* is using a siren's song to fuck with you."

I immediately scoff at that. "Oh, please. I mean, I believe in mermaids and stuff, but even *I* don't believe in sirens."

"You don't have to believe in them. I'm telling you, I think he's using the song of one to hurt you. To hypnotize you."

"I'm not hypnotized." I don't know why I feel so defensive about this, but I do. "I have an inner ear infection or something. I'll see Jonas about it, he'll have Lucy whip me up some kind of herbal concoction, and I'll be as good as new."

Xander doesn't look convinced, so I cover my eyes with my arm and take a deep breath.

"I know there's a lot of scary shit going on, but I think you're getting a little dramatic with this."

"Why are you being so stubborn about this?"

"Because the music is *amazing*, and I actually like it, and not much is going on in my life at this exact moment that I like a lot. I mean, besides you. So why can't I just enjoy it?"

"Because it's not real." Xander moves to kneel next to me and frames my face in his hands. "And because it's trying to hurt you with it. It's dangerous, Lora."

"I'll have Jonas look me over," I promise and cover his hand with mine. I hate seeing the fear and worry in his dark eyes. "Trust me, it'll be okay."

"I trust *you*." His voice is rough now. "But I don't trust *it*. And I'm telling you, it's fucking with you."

"Okay." I know he's wrong, but he's so worried, I don't want to argue with him. "Okay, we're going to figure this out. I'm sorry it has you so worried."

"I've been worried for more than a year." He sighs and rubs his forehead with his fingers. "I have an entire coven to worry about—a group of people who depend on me. What if *it* slips past me and gets to them?"

"Not possible. First of all, don't underestimate the power of every witch in that coven, Xander. And secondly, you won't let it happen."

"No pressure."

Chapter Eleven

He should have slapped her. And he would have if his power hadn't been cut off at the knees.

Now the little whore is fucking him. Their abilities have grown, and they diminish his light, *his* force. And that fills him with the rage of a thousand fires. He's unable to do more than taunt, despite all the progress he's made.

And that's another reason they'll both die.

They'll *all* die.

Very soon.

But until then, he needs to regain the strength he's lost. Tormenting them only weakens him. He needs a soul.

He has to kill.

And that makes him very, very happy.

Chapter Twelve
Xander

"Breena's already here," Lorelei announces as we walk into the restaurant that sits just across from the pier, where tourists wander down to the small lighthouse to take pictures and enjoy the ocean breeze. "And she has a...*line*. Like, people are lined up in front of her. What in the name of Zeus is she doing?"

"Let's go find out."

As we approach, I see that Giles is leaning against the wall behind Breena, a smug smile on his face as he looks on. Breena shuffles her tarot cards and chats away with Marydell, who's sitting across from her.

"This is just so *fun*," Marydell says, clapping her hands excitedly. "It's been forever since I had my cards read. I hope you have good news for me, Breena."

"I don't know why I wouldn't," Breena assures the other woman in that sweet, soothing way she has. Breena's always been the peacekeeper, the one who wants to make sure everyone is comfortable. "Even if the cards have a serious tone, there's something to learn and use from the message."

"Okay, I'm ready."

Lorelei's all smiles as she interrupts. "I'm sorry, ladies, but do you mind if we eavesdrop? If you'd rather it be private, I totally understand."

"I don't mind at all," Marydell assures her. "I know that I want to hear everyone else's readings, too. Plus, maybe you'll have additional insight, Lorelei. Two witches are always better than one."

"Four," Giles reminds her, and Marydell laughs.

"Of course."

"Here we go," Breena says, laying out a simple, seven-card spread. But as she adds cards, her face grows more somber, turning chalky white.

Lorelei swallows hard.

I stand so I can get a better look and feel my stomach tighten as my mind opens to the cards. A chill runs down my spine.

"You look so serious," Marydell says with a nervous laugh, looking around at all of us. "Am I going to lose the next election or something?"

"Of course, not," Breena says with a forced smile. She clears her throat and glances at Lorelei with eyes that scream, "*What should I tell her?*"

"I don't like that death card," Marydell says, pointing.

"Well, it doesn't always mean *death*," Breena says. "It

can mean an ending, for sure. Perhaps you'll be ending a toxic relationship, or you'll move on to another job. It could even mean that you're making some changes in your life, letting go of the past and moving forward."

"Oh, I don't actually mind that at all," Marydell replies, clearly relieved. "There are definitely some areas of my life that I could let go of."

Breena works her way through each card, giving Marydell explanations of what the cards mean and what they can potentially be referring to.

She gives no specifics.

"Well, this was fun." Marydell sits back in her chair, taking one last look at the cards before standing. "Thank you so much, Breena."

"You're welcome," Breena says.

"I'm meeting a friend out on the pier," Marydell continues, gathering her purse. "I'd better get out there, or she'll think I'm standing her up. Have a good day, all of you."

"I'm sorry, everyone," Breena says to the rest of her line. "I think I have to close up for the day. But I'll try to make it to the coffee shop real soon and do more readings then."

There's a collective sigh of disappointment as the line disperses into the restaurant, and the four of us take chairs at the round table that seats six.

"What did you see?" Giles asks when everyone is out of earshot. "For real? I never did learn tarot."

"Nothing." Breena swallows hard, staring down at

the cards. "Whenever I read for someone, I get intuitive messages from my guides, along with the messages of the cards. I'm able to weave them together to give insight. But when the spread was done, and I opened myself up, there was just *emptiness.* No message. Nothing at all."

"I felt the same," Lorelei confirms, watching the door Marydell just exited through.

"What does that mean?" Giles asks, but when he sees the look on Breena's face, he sighs. "Oh."

"I'm sorry we're late." Lucy's out of breath as she and Jonas join us and take their seats. "I got caught up in making some hawthorn berry tincture and lost track of time."

"And I was having that conversation with Louisa in Hallows End and also lost track of time," Jonas puts in. "Breena, why do you look like you've seen a ghost?"

"Because I think I have."

She relays to Lucy and Jonas what happened during her reading with Marydell.

"Maybe it was just an off reading," Lucy says, waving it off. "Sometimes, the cards just don't want to cooperate, or the guides don't want to talk."

"No," Lorelei disagrees, shaking her head. "It was definitely the right reading."

"Did I do the right thing?" Breena demands. "By not telling her what I saw and just placating her? How do you tell someone that, based on the cards, she's not likely to make it?"

"You don't," I reply simply and reach over to pat

Breena's arm. "You can't tell her that. You did the right thing, Breena. Everything can change in an instant. Maybe she takes the long way home or doesn't eat the thing that would poison her. Or, well...*anything*. You can't know for certain what the future holds because there's always free will."

"He's right," Jonas adds. "You did the right thing."

"Thank you." Breena wipes a little tear from the corner of her eye. "I've never had anything like that happen before. So weird."

"I hope it doesn't mean anything bad for her," Lucy says with a frown. "I like her so much. She's great for this town—and the witch community in general."

"I agree," Lorelei says. "I hope she stays safe."

"What did Louisa say?" I ask Jonas. "You were going to ask her about water spells and such, right?"

"Yes, I wanted to pick her brain. She kept asking me why I was curious, and I hated lying to her. She's my dearest friend."

"It's not malicious," Lorelei reminds him but then frowns and turns to me. "Wait, I didn't know you needed water spells. I have quite a few."

Jonas catches my eye, and I nod. "I asked him to ask Louisa because of the music you keep hearing, Lora. We wanted to know if she's ever heard of something like that happening to someone."

Before Lorelei can respond, Giles adds, "Plus, with *it* using the water at Breena's old place, we wanted some insight."

"Did she have some?" I ask Jonas.

"Not much," he admits, shaking his head. "I couldn't give her specifics, so everything she told me was very vague. Frustratingly so. She did mention there was some lore about sailors hearing siren songs in the old times, but she thought it was just a tale. She told me to ask my mother."

"Oh, Jonas." Lucy leans over to kiss her husband's cheek, and I feel sympathy for the other man when I see the sadness in his eyes.

His mother has been gone for three hundred years.

"My gods, how long ago is the *old times*?" Lucy asks. "If Louisa thinks it's 1692, what timeframe would the *old times* be for her?"

"A very long time ago," Jonas says with a laugh. "She also said she didn't know of any spells that could be cast to affect large bodies of water. Of course, there's no running water in Hallows End, and she wouldn't even know what that is, so I couldn't ask her about a town's water source."

"I've been doing some reading." All eyes turn to me. "Whatever this is, it's not mentioned in anything I've researched."

"Of course, not," Breena mutters darkly. "It's like it's an overachiever or something. It's ridiculous."

"Agreed," Lucy says with a long sigh. "Xander, did you call a coven meeting yet?"

"No. Sorry, I forgot. I'll do that for this weekend. My mom and grandma will be here."

Jonas's eyes narrow, and the others smile with excitement.

"Oh, that'll be a wonderful surprise for everyone," Breena says. "I've really missed your mother and Miss Sandra."

"They're excited, too."

"This would be more relatives of mine?" Jonas asks quietly.

"They are, yes. I've told them about you and tried to explain the best I could. They're both eager to meet you. Grandma says she's bringing some things to give to you. I have no idea what they are."

"It'll be my pleasure to meet them."

"Boy, it sure got stormy outside."

At Giles's observation, we all turn to look out the windows that give us a view of the pier and the water. It's suddenly churning like crazy, almost sending waves up onto the pier itself. It reminds me of the outer bands of a hurricane.

And something about it has my blood running cold.

Of course, the people out there don't move. They don't flee and run for safety, leaving the pier for shelter.

They just pull out their phones to capture it all.

"I don't like that," I murmur, narrowing my eyes. I don't want to alarm the others, but something is very wrong. "I want a closer look."

"Xander, I don't know if we should go out there."

"I'll fly over it," I reply, already walking away from the table. I can feel the others walking behind me as I push through the door. The wind whips through my hair, and rather than shift into the raven, I stay back to make sure the others are safe.

"Holy shit, this is hurricane-level," Giles yells.

"I'm going to fly up, just to see what's happening out there. I won't be gone long. Please, stay here. If it gets worse, go back into the restaurant."

"Be careful," Lorelei says, slipping her hand into mine. "Please, just be careful."

With a nod, I shift into the bird and take flight, looking down at what's happening below as well as trying to see what's going on out in the ocean.

About a mile offshore, everything is calm. The sun is shining. There's no storm.

Knowing for sure it's *it* who's come to stir up trouble, I circle back to the restaurant and see the others huddled around Lorelei as if they're trying to get her attention.

Her eyes are wide, and she's staring out at the tumultuous water.

She's hearing the fucking music. I know it.

As soon as I'm near the ground, I shift back into myself and hurry over to the others. "What's going on?"

"She's in some kind of a trance," Lucy says, her voice unsteady, her gaze not leaving her cousin. "Lorelei, honey, wake up."

"She's hearing the music." My voice is flat and hard as I reach out to take Lorelei's shoulders in my hands. "Lora."

Usually, that's enough to bring her out of the grasp the song has on her, but not this time.

"Baby, come out of it. Lorelei."

She shrugs me off and begins walking toward the pier. Her steps are sure and quick, and we hurry to keep up with her.

"She's *not* going into that water," Breena decrees.

"Of course, not," Jonas says, but I see what Breena does. *It* is pulling her to the churning harbor.

"Lorelei. Stop walking." She ignores my hard, demanding voice.

Just as we're halfway out to the end of the pier, an enormous wave comes up over the side and grasps Marydell, as if human fingers are plucking a kernel of popcorn out of a bucket. Then, it takes her over the side and into the water's depths.

"Oh, my goddess!" Lucy shrieks. "Marydell!"

"Lorelei!" I'm practically screaming in her ear, but it's as though she's gone deaf. She's not responding to me at all. I see she's begun to tremble as she walks, her teeth chattering. She's so pale, so *cold*, and the hold *it* has on her sends pure fury through me.

It won't take Lorelei.

As we near the end of the pier, the water splashes up once more, dumping Marydell back onto the wooden planks just feet from where we are.

The other onlookers have already fled back to safety, so it's just us with Marydell.

And Lorelei, who's still being held prisoner.

"Repeat after me," I say, then run through the hand motions for one of the most powerful banishing spells I know. "Gods, goddesses, ancestors, and guides, lend us your strength for us to make strides. Guardians protect us and shield us from harm. Angels lend weapons to take up as arms. Banish this evil, vanquish from sight, cut the cord of its sinister blight. We call on the sacred—three times three. This is our will, so mote it be!"

Everyone but Lora repeats after me, and together, we chant the spell over and over again until the water recedes and the wind dies. Lorelei shakes her head as if trying to clear it and then looks over at us with a frown.

"How did we get onto the pier? Boy, it's cold." She shivers, pulling her shawl around her tightly.

"Marydell," Lucy says, running back to the other woman lying lifeless on the platform. "Oh, goddess. Marydell, come back to us."

"Holy shit," Giles says softly, squatting next to Lucy and keeping her from touching the woman.

Marydell's eyes are stark white, her skin already gray, and the expression on her lovely face is one of terror.

"*It* terrorized her before it killed her," Breena says. "The cards were right. There was nothing in them because *she* would be nothing very soon. Oh, I should have told her. Maybe she would have gone home. I should have told her."

"It's not your fault," Giles soothes her, rubbing her back in rhythmic circles.

"I know, but it feels like it is. I was warned, and I didn't tell her."

"I don't remember anything," Lorelei admits slowly, staring down at Marydell with horrified eyes, gripping her shawl even tighter. "The six of us were going to have dinner at the restaurant, and it got so stormy while we were talking."

"You heard the music."

She blinks up at me, confused at first, and then she frowns. "Oh, you're right. I heard the music. It's so beautiful, you guys. Did you all hear it, too? Where's the band?"

"No band," Giles says grimly as he wraps his arm around Breena, tugging her against his side. "It's fucking with you, Lora. There's no music."

"No, I—"

"*Stop it*!" Lorelei's head whips around to me, clearly surprised by the harsh tone of my voice. "Just fucking stop it, Lorelei. Stop defending it. The music isn't real because *it* is messing with you. And all you do is deny it. I can't keep you safe if you won't work with me."

"Why do you want the music to be real?" Breena asks, much kinder than I could be right now.

"Because it's so beautiful," Lorelei says, then her face crumples, and she bursts into tears. "It just makes me feel so happy. It's like beautiful light flows through me every time I hear it. It's not real?"

"No, baby." I pull her to me and hold on tightly as the sun comes out, warming us. "It's not real."

Suddenly, Lorelei tears herself out of my arms and rushes over to the pier's railing, emptying her stomach over the side.

"She's always nauseated after hearing the music," I inform the others grimly as I hold her hair back for her. "It's been getting progressively worse as time goes on. At first, she was just a little queasy, but now, well...it's this."

"Why did it kill Marydell?" Lucy wants to know. "What could it have possibly wanted with that sweet woman? She's never hurt anyone."

"The energy," Jonas replies. "The power. And for the fun of it. We all know *it* doesn't care if it hurts someone who's good."

"I have to call the authorities," Giles says, pulling his phone out of his pocket, but there are already sirens, and they don't sound far away.

"Someone already did," I reply. "How in the hell do we explain this?"

"We don't," Lucy says. "She was washed out by the water and somehow got tossed back. That's all we know. It's not a lie. It's exactly what we and everyone else on the pier saw."

"That's fucked-up," Giles says. "It's just all so fucked-up."

"**I**'m not going back home," Lorelei declares. We're all sitting in my living room, just an hour after the whole ordeal, trying to calm down together. Breena made tea with valerian root, which is excellent for calming, and the aunts dropped off some soup, but none of us has been ready to eat anything yet.

"What do you mean?" I ask Lorelei with a frown.

"Just what I said. The water scares me now. It's not safe for me, and if it's not safe for *me*, that means you're all in danger. I won't have anything happening to any of you because of me. So, until this is all over, I stay inland."

"I understand what you're saying," Breena says slowly, thinking it over. "But, Lorelei, you gain the most power by being near the water."

"Not anymore. Or, at least, not right now. I get physically sick and am apparently hearing ghost music that puts me under some kind of fucked-up spell. We have too much to do, and all *it* wants is to scare and distract me. It's working. I'm going to take that piece of his power off our plate. Xander and I will stay here. And before you ask, yes, it pisses me off more than you know. I miss my shoreline already, but this is just how it has to be for now. We'll destroy this piece of trash, and then life can go back to normal."

"I think you're right." This comes from Jonas, who's watching Lorelei with narrowed eyes. "It's all a distraction. Removing that piece will certainly anger *it*, but it will be an advantage for us. It's less power it can use."

"I'm fine with us staying here." I reach over to rub Lora's thigh. "Do you want to go home to get your things?"

"No." She shakes her head stubbornly. "I'm not going anywhere near there. But I *will* need some clothes, my computer, and my notes. And there's food in the fridge that shouldn't go to waste."

"I'll go." I kiss her head softly. "I'll go pack up your things and the food."

"I can help," Lucy offers and then turns to Jonas, who nods. "We can both help."

"When do your mom and grandmother arrive?" Giles asks me.

"Friday afternoon. Two more days."

"We really need that coven meeting," he responds.

I glance over at Lucy. "Can you help me get the word out?"

"Of course. I'll get the aunts to help. Saturday morning?"

"Friday night," I counter. "Mom and Grandma should arrive at around four in the afternoon. Let's set the meeting for six."

"Great." Lucy steps out of the room, her phone already pressed to her ear.

"How is the tapestry coming?" Lorelei asks Breena.

"I only have a couple of rows left." Breena beams with happiness. "It's *so close.* I'll have it finished by early next week."

"Excellent," Jonas says. "Good work, Breena."

"Thanks. I'm so relieved it's almost finished. I don't think I'll do any kind of weaving ever again."

"I don't blame you," Lorelei replies. "I think it's time we get a plan in place. For lifting the curse and destroying that son of a bitch."

"The aunts are on it," Lucy announces as she walks back into the room. "They're calling everyone. We're going to meet at their house, as usual."

"Thank you."

Lucy smiles at me. "That was easy."

Her smile falters when she looks out the window to the street beyond.

"What is it?"

I turn to follow her gaze, but I don't see anything.

"Nothing," she says, frowning. "I thought I saw something, but it must have just been a shadow or a reflection."

"Not another corpse," Lorelei mutters, standing to look outside. Last year, while in this very room, the women all saw a zombie standing out in the street, watching us. "I don't see anything."

"My mind is just overactive," Lucy says with a sigh. "Every little noise and every shadow freaks me out."

"I think that's normal," Breena says in that soothing way she has. "We're all on edge. And I think we should be. I don't want any of us being caught unawares."

"You're right." I nod over at her and then glance down at Lorelei. "Are you feeling better?"

"Physically? Yes, I'm better. I won't be upchucking again. But emotionally? I'm a little strung out."

"Sounds about right," Giles says with a grin. "I'm no professional, but I think you *should* be."

"You need some rest," Lucy tells her.

"I need to kick some ass."

Chapter Thirteen
Lorelei

T*he music. Goddess, it's so beautiful. It softly tinkles like little bells on the wind, and then the flutes and wind instruments join until the sweetest voice I've ever heard builds over the water.*

I can't understand what it's saying. Perhaps it's a different language? It sounds like it could be Gaelic, which just adds to the intrigue and beauty for me. Whatever language it is, it's absolutely amazing.

I want to step inside the music. I want it to surround and consume me, to just fill me up until I'm bursting with it. Until it's coming out of my fingers and toes, shooting out of the ends of my hair. It feels like I should be able to dance within it and wear it like a soft, comforting blanket.

I absolutely do not *want it to end.*

I love that I hear it at the shore. The water is my place, it's my element, and the music only makes it more special.

It makes it feel like it's only mine, like it's made just for me, which makes me long for it even more.

I don't actually know where I am right now. I can feel the sand and rocks under my feet, and once in a while, the cool water licks up and over my skin, filling me with energy. I'm on a shoreline somewhere, but it's dark enough outside that I can't tell exactly where I am.

The sky flashes with lightning, illuminating the water and land as bright as day for about two seconds before disappearing. I know where I am now. I'm on the shoreline near my cottage. Knowing that I'm so close to home makes me feel even better.

The lightning streaks once more, and then a scene begins to move across the clouds and sky above the water as if it's a giant movie screen with the music as its soundtrack.

At first, it's absolutely wonderful. I see Breena and Lucy with me, all of us as children. We're standing on our quilt, hands clasped as we spin little spells and smile happily.

I see my mom and the aunts, Agatha still living, bustling about their kitchen to make dinner for all of us. They're laughing and joking, and Agatha tosses a handful of flour at Hilda, covering all of them in white.

I want to jump in there and join in the pure joy radiating from that room. Oh, how I miss the three of them together.

Then the scene shifts, and I see the six of us, my cousins and our men, in Xander's home. It's as though I'm standing on the street, looking into the house, watching as I walk to the window and stare out. I look afraid.

Breena and Lucy join me, and they appear frightened, too.

"There's nothing to be scared of," I yell to them, wishing they could hear me. "Everything is wonderful. Don't worry."

But they shake their heads, and Xander pulls them away from the glass as if to protect them.

The sky grows dark, then lightning streaks across the expanse again before another scene begins.

This one is not a good memory.

First, I see Aunt Agatha hanging in the kitchen of her little house, not quite lifeless. She struggles against the rope, clawing and kicking, crying out to be let go. A shadow sits in the corner, laughing at her as she dies.

I fall to my knees, sobbing as I watch my sweet aunt die. And then the shadow leaves, and as if someone put the film on fast-forward, the sun comes up, and Lucy walks into the room, looking for her mama.

She struggles to cut Agatha down and folds her into her lap, weeping as she holds her mother's lifeless body.

Lightning flashes again, and the scene changes once more. In this one, I'm walking through a forest, and all the people I love are hanging from the trees, their hands tied behind their backs, already dead.

As I pass them, they stare at me with wide, empty eyes, and I can hear their souls crying out.

"Why didn't you save us?"

As lightning flashes once more, I press my hands to my mouth. Goddess, I don't want to see any more. But suddenly, I'm thrust into a tiny village that looks like the reenactment village near Salem, where tourists can go to see how the Puritans lived.

But this is no reenactment village.

"Hallows End?" I murmur. "This is Hallows End."

A circle of witches sits around a fire, with Jonas standing and holding a Book of Shadows, speaking loudly while the others chant and toss herbs into the fire.

He's casting the curse of the blood moon.

I don't know how I know that for sure, but I do. After it's cast, the film speeds up, showing me the next three hundred years in fast-forward. I see people age and die.

I see a witch die every year.

Finally, I see Jonas with Lucy.

The lightning flashes, showing me absolute despair and devastation.

Hallows End is on fire, and all the people who live there are dead.

My mother and Hilda hang in their tiny kitchen.

And the six of us are tied to stakes, burning.

"No!" My voice is hoarse from weeping as I stand and scream. "This will not happen! We'll defeat you!"

But the music is back, and it slides over me like a soothing balm.

"No," I call out again. "No."

"It's okay."

I shake my head and gasp, realizing that Xander's holding me.

"It's too dark."

With the flick of his finger, several candles light around the room, casting a gentle glow.

"Oh, goddess."

I bury my face in his chest and cry. So much anger and grief come pouring out of me. I know it's not just about what I saw in that nightmare. It's *everything*. Losing our baby, lashing out at Xander, leaving Salem for so long...

Everything that's happened since I returned home. Losing our sweet Agatha and living in fear of *it*.

It all just pours out of me as I sob against this strong, comforting, and amazing man who holds me so patiently, so tenderly. His big hands rub up and down my back, and I feel him kissing my hair, murmuring sweetly that everything will be okay. *I'm* going to be okay. I'd forgotten how easy it is to believe him in moments like these. Xander is my rock. He's the best part of my life. Our souls are connected in ways I can't even begin to explain or comprehend, I just know I'm so much better when I'm with him than when I fight it and am away from him.

Finally, the tears fade, and I take a long, shaky breath.

"Bad dream?" Xander asks with a small smile as I pull back and wipe my face with the tissues he offers me. The look in his eyes is so...*tender*. That's the word that keeps popping into my head to describe what I see, and it's really the most accurate. Xander is a big man, and he can be an incredibly dangerous one, but to me, he's never been anything but gentle.

"Yeah." I blow my nose and take a deep breath. "Horrifying, actually."

"You were so upset," he murmurs, wiping away the rest of my tears. "You were crying out in your sleep, and I couldn't wake you up. It scared me."

"I heard the music," I admit softly, still sniffling as I stare at his Adam's apple. "And then it showed me everything as if I were watching a movie."

As Xander listens silently, I tell him everything I saw and am surprised by how much I actually remember. When I finish, the look on his gorgeous face is at once so incredibly sad that it breaks my heart, and full of stone-cold rage.

"He's been fucking with you for weeks, and it's done. As of right now."

"We've already put up wards and protections. I don't know what else we can do."

"I know of one more spell." He drags his fingertips down my cheek. "But you may not be up for it tonight, and that's perfectly okay."

"What kind of spell?"

"A sex spell."

I narrow my eyes at him. "Is this some kind of trick to get me to have sex with you? Because I'll do that without the trickery."

He doesn't laugh, but his eyes are full of humor as he

leans in to kiss my cheek. "No trick. You know it's not. Sex between soulmates added to a protection spell is incredibly powerful."

"I know." I laugh, already feeling so much better. "I just had to give you a hard time. Because it totally sounds like a line."

"I guess it does. If you don't feel up to it, we can do it in the morning."

"Just give me a second." I kiss him quickly and then climb from the bed to pad into the bathroom. I need to splash some water on my face to clear my head all the way. I want to be fully present for this spell.

And for Xander.

I shed the T-shirt and panties I wore to bed and toss them into the hamper. Then, wearing nothing but what the gods gave me, I return to the bedroom.

He's lying on his side, head propped on his hand, all aglow in the candlelight. And, to my utter amusement, he crooks a finger at me.

"Over here."

"I mean, I planned to come over there." I walk very slowly and watch with satisfaction as his eyes travel lazily down my nude body. "But now that you're all bossy, I think I'll take my time."

He smirks, and with his long arms, simply reaches out and snatches me around the waist to tumble me back onto the bed.

"There." He seems quite happy with himself as he

kisses me, long and slow. Our legs tangle, and I can feel that he's already hard and ready for me.

Of course, he's *always* ready for me. That was never an issue with Xander.

He kisses my forehead and then my nose, moving his hand down my ribs to my hip.

"As much fun as this is," I whisper before biting his chin—just because I can, "we have to remember that we have a goal here."

"Right." That hand drifts over my ass, and his long fingers skim the very outside of my labia, making me suck in a sharp breath. "Goals. Got it."

"Huh?"

He laughs and pushes me onto my back, then links our fingers and braces my hand above my head as his mouth does delicious things to my neck.

"This is going to be slow," he whispers into my ear. "And we're going to chant the spell over and over again, together."

"I don't know the words."

"I'll teach you." So much promise hangs in those words. "Look at me, baby."

I didn't even realize I'd closed my eyes.

"It's not a long spell," he continues.

"Some of the most powerful incantations are the short ones." I can't help but sigh when he drags his cock along my wet folds. "How in the hell am I supposed to concentrate?"

There's that sly smile again. "We'll make it work. Goddess, you're unbelievable, Lorelei."

He's always been vocal during sex. *Always*. So, he'll have no issue at all with speaking the spell.

I, on the other hand, am mostly good at making sounds. I can't even remember my name when he's inside me.

"Focus, sweetheart."

I open my eyes again and work to keep them trained on him as he slides so effortlessly, so smoothly, inside of me.

"Xander."

"I know." He kisses me softly. "We've got this."

"Damn right, we do. All right, what do we say?"

"You can repeat each line after me, okay?"

I nod and bite my lip when he pulls back, just until only the head of his cock is seated inside of me.

"Here we go." He's still holding my hand, his eyes on mine, and goddess knows he's cradling my heart inside his. I've never felt closer to him than I do right now. "Heart to heart, soul to soul, two as one, our power grows. Mind to mind and skin to skin, our power soars, let it begin. Heart and soul, mind and flesh, only us, our auras mesh."

He prompts each line, and then I repeat them. Finally, once I've memorized it, we begin chanting it together. The flames of the candles grow around us as the energy in the room increases. We're speaking slowly at first, Xander's movements matching the tempo, and then it all starts to grow. The words, the thrusts, and our breaths become a fire all on their own.

He doesn't miss a beat in the words, but when Xander can see that I'm ready to fall apart, he nods, urging me on. I succumb to wave after wave of pure emotion and sensation rolling through me.

I'm incredibly proud that I keep it together enough to continue the spell with him, and then he's coming, too, finishing just as we utter the spell for the last time.

The wind calms, the flames return to their normal strength, and we're left a panting, sweaty mess in the middle of his huge bed, grinning at each other.

"That felt like a mating spell," I inform him.

"It's both." He flops onto his side to spare me from his weight and tries to catch his breath. "It's a protection mating spell."

"It was intense." I fling my arm over my eyes, chest still heaving. "Goddess, it was intense. How have we never done that before?"

"We didn't need it before." He turns his head to look at me. "And I didn't know about it before."

"How do you know about it now?"

"I read about it in Jonas's sister's grimoire."

"Wow, that's a three-hundred-year-old spell?"

"At least."

"That's pretty cool." My heart and breath are starting to calm down finally, and the air is chilly on my skin, so I pull the covers over us.

"Do you feel any better?"

I'm quiet as I listen to the house around us. It feels...
settled. "I think so. It's almost as if we just erected a big
bubble around us."

"I like our bubble."

I grin as I glide my fingers down his arm. "Me, too."

"You're here!"

My mom bursts out of her door with
Hilda hot on her heels. They both envelop
Xander's mom, Shelly, and his grandma, Sandra, into big
hugs.

"What am I, chopped liver?"

Mom grins at me over Shelly's shoulder. "Right now?
Yes. Oh, my dear friend, it's so good to lay eyes on you."

"You, too," Shelly replies and then turns to hug
Hilda. "You both look fabulous."

"Did you try my anti-aging spell?" Sandra asks them.
"Because neither of you has aged a day."

"That, and some carrot oil around the eyes," Mom
replies. "Thank you for coming before the rest of the
coven arrives. I needed a little time with you."

"We wouldn't have it any other way," Sandra assures
her as we all go inside the house and sit around the
kitchen table. Jonas, Lucy, Breena, and Giles are already
here, looking happy and full of the delicious gingersnap
cookies Hilda made, which are sitting in the middle of
the table. Lucy and Breena even brought their familiars,

who are snuggled up together under the table. "Now, I know the others, but I don't know you. That would make you Jonas, my many, many times great-uncle."

Jonas smiles as he climbs to his feet and gently hugs the older woman, then he turns to Shelly and gives her a hug, as well.

"I'm not used to meeting family," he confesses. If I'm not mistaken, I see tears gathering at the corners of his eyes. "It's truly my pleasure to meet you."

"Sit," Sandra says, waving him into his seat. "Let's all sit and have a nice chat. Of course, Xander has filled us in on most of what's been going on, but I like to get the stories firsthand. So, I want you all to start at the beginning and tell us *everything*."

"That's going to be a long story," Lucy warns her.

"Well, we just so happen to have tea, cookies, and time," Sandra assures her. "Go on. Tell us."

Goddess, I love Xander's grandmother. Both of these women are special to me. As witches, they're wise and gifted, and I can learn so much from them. As *women*, they're kind and have been friends with the aunts since they were all children.

With Shelly living in Florida, and the loss of Agatha, my mom and Hilda have felt as if they're missing two limbs.

Suddenly, in the middle of Breena telling her story about not wanting to live in her house, Shelly looks up at the kitchen doorway, and her face breaks out into a wide smile.

"Oh, my friend. I've missed you."

I follow her gaze and see Agatha standing there, plain as the rest of us. She's smiling back at Shelly.

"I miss you, too," Agatha says, surprising me. She doesn't usually say much; she generally just hovers around.

"*I* miss you, too, but you won't show yourself to me," Lucy reminds her mother, who just shrugs in the doorway.

"Anyway, keep going," Shelly says to Breena. "And, for the record, I wouldn't spend another minute in that house either."

It takes us close to an hour to get through everything that's happened, including the incident with Marydell just a few days ago.

"You've all been busy," Sandra murmurs, watching Xander through narrowed eyes. "You didn't tell us you were possessed and nearly killed."

"No reason to worry you."

"And that, my dear boy," Shelly says, leaning forward, "is bullshit."

We all snicker, and Xander has the decency to look chastised.

"Now that we're up to date, we'll be ready for the coven meeting," Sandra says, nodding her head before turning back to Jonas. "I want you to know that, while I understand I can never take the place of your mother or your grandmother, you are my family, and I will happily fill that role for you if and when you need it. I see that

Xander gave you your mother's wedding ring to give to Lucy. It suits her."

"Thank you." Jonas shifts in his seat, obviously not entirely comfortable. I've never seen the man nervous before, and it's fascinating. "Do you know much about my family? I know it was so long ago, and it surprised me that Xander had her ring. I don't know how it survived."

"It was passed down through Katrina to her children and so on, until it came to me," Shelly says. "When I divorced Xander's father, I put the ring back in the box that had been given to me and gave it to my son. It's an heirloom, and I wanted it to be in the family. Of course, it went through quite the cleansing ritual."

Shelly leans over to pat Lucy's shoulder.

"No need to worry about bad juju being attached to the ring, darling."

"I know there's not," Lucy says with a soft smile. "I would feel it if there were."

"I really only know what I've read in the family grimoires and what's been told to me through the years about your immediate family, Jonas," Sandra continues. "But I do have something for you."

She fishes around in her handbag, which is big enough to swim in, then pulls out a spell jar, a rose quartz sphere, and a bottle of sage, all before finding what she's looking for.

"Ah, here it is." Sandra sets her bag back on the floor and passes Jonas a flat brown box that has clearly seen better days.

He opens it, and then his eyes fly back to Sandra's.

"What is it?" I ask, trying to see over the flap of the box.

"Letters," he says quietly. He has to swallow to continue speaking. "From my mother to my sister."

"There are about twenty of them there," Sandra confirms. "And I believe they were sent while your sister was in hiding in Boston during the hysteria. I don't have the letters that Katrina sent back to her, but—"

"This is absolutely incredible," Jonas says. "I can never repay you for this."

"They belong to you," Shelly replies simply. "And I suspect it'll be nice to hear—or at least read—your mother's voice for the first time in so long."

"You have no idea." Jonas looks up at both women. "Katrina and my mother would like you both very much."

"And I know that we would like them," Sandra says.

Breena sniffles, and her mother passes her a tissue. "This is just the sweetest thing."

"Oh, sweet Breena," Shelly says with a smile. "Since we couldn't make it up for the wedding a few months ago, I brought wedding gifts with me."

"Gifts?" Giles asks. "As in, more than one?"

"Of course," Shelly replies. "You're our babies. We've known you your whole lives, and we share the family of the coven. Did you think we wouldn't spoil you senseless?"

"I've missed you both so much," Breena says, tears still falling. "You coming here is the only gift I need."

"I think we'll be moving back," Sandra declares, and Shelly stares at her mother in shock.

"But Florida is better for your arthritis," Shelly says.

"But Salem is better for my soul, and that's what matters. Besides, this young man needs a grandmother."

"Hi," Xander says, waving at his grandma. "I'm still here, you know."

"Don't start getting jealous now," Sandra says with a laugh. "There's plenty of me to go around. Now we have to go house hunting."

"There's room here," Hilda offers. "At least while you're getting settled and looking for a more permanent place. You know we'd love to have you with us."

"Yes," Sandra says with a delighted grin. "It's much better for my soul."

CHAPTER FOURTEEN

He's so *strong*. So powerful. Yes, killing that ridiculous woman and pulling her energy was the right decision. In doing so, he gained almost all the energy he needs to incarnate and kill every witch in Salem if he wants to.

And yes, he wants to.

They all deserve to die.

Perhaps there's no need to wait until Samhain to get the job done. He heard them talking about the coven meeting, and what better time to destroy them all than the present? They'll be together.

It's as if the universe has choreographed the perfect opportunity for him. And if that's the case, if the gods themselves are gifting him this moment, it would be disrespectful not to take advantage of their offer.

Excitement fills him, fueling the adrenaline he's been

running on since he sucked the soul out of the woman they called Marydell.

Today is the day.

CHAPTER FIFTEEN
XANDER

"This apple cider is absolutely divine," Mom says before taking another delicate sip. "Percy, you always made the best cider in Salem."

"I'm glad you think so, Shelly." The older man looks pleased as others in the group agree that his cider is, indeed, the best around. "I brought extra bottles in case anyone would like to take some home."

I love my coven. They're as much my family as my mother and grandmother, and I've been their leader since Grandma moved to Florida. I didn't think I would be chosen to lead, but it was unanimous among the witches that they wanted me to be the one to guide them. I was so honored, I readily agreed.

There have been moments when I've wondered if I made the right choice.

Particularly in the past year.

But I know, without a doubt, that if I asked any of them, they'd say they made the right decision, which fills me with pride.

I love them, and they love me. Without question.

"Before we go," Giles's mom says, turning to Breena, "what is the progress report on the tapestry? I don't mean to put any pressure on you, of course. I'm just curious."

"You guys." Breena sighs and suddenly looks defeated and so forlorn. "I forgot to tell you. It was going great, coming along at a wonderful pace, but then the loom broke, and I haven't been able to fix it. Of course, I immediately ordered a new one, but it won't be here for another week or so. I'll still be able to finish by Samhain, I promise that won't change, but it's put me behind."

"I have a loom you can use," Margaret Sanders chimes in. "I'm certainly not using it. In fact, we'll go home and fetch it right now and bring it over to your place, Breena."

"Oh, are you sure you don't mind?" Breena's face lights up with hope. I know she's feeling so much pressure to get the tapestry done in time. She's been working tirelessly for more than six months on the project.

"Absolutely not," Margaret assures her. "It's no trouble at all."

"I hope everyone plans to attend the Samhain ball tomorrow evening," Hilda says with a bright smile. "The committee almost canceled it out of respect for our sweet friend, Marydell, but she would have wanted us to move forward with the festivities. This was her favorite part of the year."

"She always denied being a witch, but there was some magic there," Grandma says with a wise nod.

"I'm so happy we're here in time for it. Samhain itself is still almost two weeks away," Mom adds.

"So many things are happening in Salem this month, the committee decided to throw the ball a little early this year," Astrid says. "And that works just fine for me because this is my favorite time of year, too, and that means we get to celebrate longer."

"Percy?" Mom's voice is tentative as she watches the man. When I follow her gaze, I feel my blood run cold.

Percy's eyes have gone white, and he's sitting perfectly still in his chair, his back straight despite the usual curve in his shoulders, his hands on his thighs. His lips move as if he's speaking, but no sound comes out. His face is almost blue, as if he's hypothermic, and it looks as though his salt-and-pepper hair is turning grayer by the second.

"*It*'s here," Jonas says calmly, tilting his head to the side as if he's curious about what's happening but not at all bothered.

I know what he's doing.

It wants us to freak out.

"It would seem so." I glance around the circle and speak to everybody telepathically. I know not everyone can hear me, but they'll know. *Do not react.*

Some nod. Others narrow their eyes.

Astrid raises her eyebrow as if to say, "*The audacity!*" and it almost makes me want to smile.

The sky darkens. Not just as if a storm blew over, but as if night fell in an instant. Suddenly, we're plunged into blackness.

With the flick of several wrists, fires ignite around the backyard, illuminating the area, and I can tell by the sound of thunder above us that we just pissed it off.

I don't give a fuck.

"As above and so below…"

"I call on the wind and the fire…"

"Lilith, hear my prayer…"

"Ancestors and guides, I call on thee…"

Every person here begins their own protection spell, something personal to them that they use on a daily basis to keep themselves safe.

I join in and take Lorelei's hand in mine as she recites her own spell.

The wind picks up, whipping and lashing about. I can't tell if it's from the power of the coven or a temper tantrum from *it*.

Percy's head whips back so unnaturally that I think his head might snap off.

"Louder," I command, feeling satisfaction when they do just that. The spells are louder, more demanding, and much more aggressive. I can feel the ancestors and deities around us, helping us.

The air is charged with magic, so tangible I can feel it slipping and sliding over my skin.

Just as quickly as it began, the sky clears, the wind disappears, and Percy collapses to the ground.

As several witches hurry to tend to the older man, I scan the yard, my mind reaching out and looking for any remnants of *it*, making sure there's no trace.

"It's gone."

I nod and glance over at Giles, who's breathing hard. He's a bit pale, his usually styled hair a tangled nest.

Then, I glance around to see that we're all a mess.

But we're whole.

"It took balls for it to attack when we're together as a coven," Giles's father says as he stands over Percy while Jonas tends to the older coven member, his mouth pressed into a grim line.

"It's because of what he did to Marydell," Hilda says. "The energy replenished him—it?—whatever we're calling it, and it made him brave."

"He won't be brave for a little while now," Jonas says. "We injured him. But he's not gone forever."

"It's not injured," Lorelei says, slowly shaking her head. "It was just playing with us. Testing us. Sure, we were stronger than it expected, but it could have done much more damage than what it did."

We discuss strategy, protection, and being vigilant.

By the time everyone walks to their cars to head for home, Percy is as good as new if a little shaken by the experience.

And when it's just the core group of us again with

our parents, Giles asks, "How much time do we really have to kill the son of a bitch?"

"It's going to try to take a life on Samhain," Sandra reminds him.

"It doesn't have to wait for that anymore," Lucy adds. "It murdered Marydell, and it wasn't even close to the festival. I don't think there will be a waiting period this year. It could be anytime."

"Agreed." I nod grimly. "I want everyone to stick together. Always. No one goes anywhere alone. It's too dangerous."

I turn to Jonas and feel a pang in my chest.

"I wish someone could go to Hallows End with you. I don't even feel like that's safe."

"I can go with him," Lucy says, but Jonas is already shaking his head. "Listen to me. I *can* go with you. I can hide in the trees, or at your house, but I don't think you should go alone. Xander's right, it's just not safe for you —for any of us—to be alone. You're my husband. Our family. You're not expendable."

Jonas tugs Lucy into his arms and holds her tightly, kissing her head before nodding as he looks around the backyard at the rest of us.

"Thank you. You've become *my* family, and I don't want anything to happen to any of you, either." He looks down at his wife and hooks a piece of her hair behind her ear. "You can come with me, but we need to be very careful."

"Of course. I know the drill."

"And that means that you don't go to work alone," Breena tells Giles, who scowls. "I'll take the loom to the shop and work there with you. I know it's too busy this time of year for you to close up for a few weeks."

"I can live with that compromise," Giles says and kisses Breena's forehead.

"I just love that you're all in love," Mom says with a happy sigh. "It's so lovely to watch. Isn't it, Mama?"

"They're absolutely adorable," Grandma agrees and then turns those shrewd eyes to me. "And I see that you two are finally figuring yourselves out."

I simply narrow my eyes at her, but Lorelei grins.

"We're getting there." She nods with a smile.

"You all should stay for dinner," Hilda says. "I won't take no for an answer. We have some soup simmering on the burner, homemade bread, and two apple pies for dessert. There's plenty of food."

"And we can make it stretch with a little magic," Astrid adds.

"You don't have to talk us into it," Mom says, hooking her arm through Giles's mom's. "Oh, I want to hear about everything that's been going on lately."

All the parents, including Giles's dad, go inside. The six of us hang back.

"I want to go check on my house," Breena says, surprising us.

"Why?" I ask her.

"We haven't been back since we discovered the water

inside, and my guides are *screaming* at me to look in on it."

"Then that's what we'll do. We can knock that out while they're all in there, fixing dinner and gossiping," Lorelei says. "I'll run in and let them know."

She jogs off to go inside and then comes running back just a few seconds later.

"Good to go," she says.

"You all ride together. I'm going to fly."

"We're not supposed to be alone, remember?" Breena points out. "That includes you, Xander. Remember what happened at Beltane when you were alone? You're not impervious to this."

"She's right," Jonas says. "You should stick with us."

"Please, don't go alone." Lorelei slips her hand into mine and holds on tightly. "It's not worth the risk."

I can't resist her.

"Okay, let's go together."

"I didn't realize your house was at the top of a hill," Giles says to Breena as we get out of the car, about fifty yards away from the house. We can't get any closer.

It's completely surrounded by water.

"It's not," she says miserably. "It's actually in a valley. My goddess, what's happening? *Why* is this happening?"

The house is submerged up to the windows. It looks

old and weathered, with part of the roof caving in on one side.

It appears far worse than it did just a few days ago.

"It looks like the energy of the house is fueling this psycho," Giles says, scowling behind his dark-rimmed glasses.

"Breena worked some powerful magic in there," Lucy reminds us. "She made products for customers, and her personal magic is incredibly strong. Of course, some of that lives on inside the house, especially with her belongings still in there."

"Well, that's creepy as fuck," Lorelei mutters. "We can't go in there. Absolutely not. I won't even reach out psychically to look around."

"No," Breena agrees, reaching for both Lorelei and Lucy and hugging them to her. "No, we won't be going back in. It's lost to us for now, and when all of this is over, I plan to tear it down and have it taken away. I'll sell the land."

"I'm so sorry, Breen." Lucy kisses Breena's cheek as the three women look at what used to be Breena's home.

"I'm not." Breena shakes her head. "I'm not sorry. Because I have a home with Giles, and our house is beautiful and perfect for us. I'm exactly where I'm supposed to be. I'm finished grieving this house and what might have been in it. Mostly, I'm pissed off that *it* decided it could take it over and mess with all of us, using something I used to love against us."

"She's so fucking amazing," Giles breathes, watching his wife with the other girls.

"You're supposed to think that." I grin and clap him on the shoulder. "You're a damn lucky man."

"Breena is the sweetest person I've ever known, although I'd say we're all particularly lucky," Jonas says with a smile. "Those three women are unlike anything I've ever seen in my long life. And, as your grandmother pointed out, you and Lorelei seem happy. I know I haven't known you long, but I've never seen you so content."

"I don't believe in *better halves*. You know how they say, 'She's my better half?' Yeah, I don't believe that because we're whole people by ourselves. But she's the best part of every day. My life doesn't work without her in it. If I didn't know better, I'd say she hung the moon."

"Maybe she did," Giles says with a grin, but then the water begins to rise around the house. "And that means we're out of here."

"Come." I take Lorelei's arm as Jonas and Giles do the same with Lucy and Breena. "We need to go."

"I'm hungry," Lucy says, not at all reacting to what's going on at the house. "Let's go eat."

"I promised Breena and Lucy we'd all get ready for the ball together," Lorelei says the next morning over pancakes. She smears so much butter and syrup over hers, I'm surprised she doesn't go into sugar shock. "So, I'll head over there in about an hour, but I have to swing by my house to get my dress and shoes."

"I'll go with you."

"I figured you'd say that. I want to check on things anyway. And if I start to go into some kind of weird trance, you have my permission to knock me out cold."

"That seems a little extreme, but duly noted."

She grins at me and pops another bite of pancake into her mouth. Aside from the night she had the nightmare, she hasn't heard the music at all, and the respite from it has been good for her.

She's been much more herself these past few days.

After her last bite of pancake, she lifts her plate to her mouth and licks the last of the butter and syrup off it, then sets it back down and licks her lips.

"Would you like to simply suck the syrup out of the bottle?"

"Don't tempt me." She laughs and then stands to load the dishwasher. "What are you wearing tonight?"

"Clothes."

She rolls her eyes and shoves her plate into the rack. "Specifically, *which* clothes are you going to wear?"

"I have a suit. I'll wear that. Why, what are you wearing?"

"You don't get to know until later."

"Then why did I have to tell you what I'm wearing?"

"Because I asked." She shuts the dishwasher, sets it to wash, and walks over to me to kiss my cheek.

I pull her down onto my lap, making her laugh.

"I love it when we're like this," she says, wrapping her arms around my neck.

"Like what?"

"*Normal.* Silly. Having fun. Enjoying pancakes."

"Could you taste the pancakes through all the sugar?"

"See? It's fun when we're like this and not worried about...other things."

"I agree." I kiss her nose and cuddle her closer. "We'll have many more moments just like this."

"I hope so. Shelly and Sandra are so wonderful. I love that they're here and are moving home. Was that a spur-of-the-moment decision on your grandmother's part?"

"It sounded like it. Mom looked shocked, but in a good way. I'll be glad to have them close so I can keep an eye on them, and because I miss them."

"The aunts will be beside themselves. They were always best friends with your mom, and having her back full time will mean the band's back together. I think it's awesome."

"I know. That's how I was able to see you so often."

"Aww, that's so sweet." She grins and kisses me, pressing her breasts to my chest. "You know, we have some free time before I have to meet up with the girls."

"Really?"

She nods with wide, innocent eyes. She's totally faking that.

"What do you suggest we do with that time?"

She crooks her finger as if she has a secret to tell me, so I bend down, and she cups her hand around my ear. "I think you should fuck me into the mattress until I can't remember my name."

I immediately stand with her in my arms and march up the stairs to the bedroom.

"You don't have to ask me twice, sweetheart."

CHAPTER SIXTEEN
LORELEI

"Thank you." I grin at Xander as he passes me the dress—safe in a green garment bag—and shoes that he just fetched from my cottage. We ended up having way too much fun in the bedroom, and I was running late getting over to Breena's house, where my two cousins were already waiting for me. "Was everything okay over there?"

"Looked normal to me," he confirms before leaning in to kiss me. "Nothing touched. I'd say it's safe."

"Good. That's good news. I might still stop by after the ball, just to see for myself."

"We can do that. I'd better go. I have some errands to run for my mom, and then I'll be getting ready, too. I'll pick you up later. Just text me when you're ready."

"Sounds good. Tell your mom hi for me."

He kisses me once more, bending me backward as he grabs my ass.

"Seriously," Lucy says from behind us. "We have to do our hair now. Go away, Xander."

He grins against my lips. "I'm being tossed out."

"Don't take it personally." I pat his chest and then wave when he leaves, turning to Lucy. She doesn't look annoyed at all. She's smiling at me. "I have it *bad.*"

"I love it so much," she says with an excited smile. "It's the way it should be, Lora. You two are just..." She makes a *chef's kiss* motion, and it makes me grin.

"We are, aren't we?"

"Where are you guys?" Breena calls out from upstairs. "My hair is going to get frizzy, and then I'll have to start all over."

"Come on." I lead the way up the stairs, carrying my garment bag and shoes. "I promised Breena I'd curl her hair."

"You have the magic touch with curls," Lucy agrees as we walk into Breena's bedroom, where our cousin waits, hands on her perfectly curvy hips, tapping her toe. "Wow, you're *never* impatient."

"I know, and I'm sorry, but my hair will dry," Breena explains. "And then I'll have to wet it again, and it's perfect right *now.*"

"Let's do this." I gesture for Breena to sit in the chair we brought up from the dining room and reach for my already preheated curling wand that dries as it curls. After sectioning out her hair, I start twirling the hair around the hot wand. "Let me just say, Xander had better *not* have looked in my garment bag. I want the dress to be a surprise."

"The man's psychic," Lucy reminds me, her voice dry as the Sahara. "He likely already knows what it looks like."

"He could never read me." I gently let a curl fall before gathering up more hair for another. "And I can't read him. I know there are spells we could do so we have a link to each other, like you and Jonas did, Luce, but I kind of like being surprised. And I like surprising *him*. It's fun. I don't want to always know what he's thinking. Besides, he's so intense sometimes, I think knowing all his thoughts would totally overwhelm me."

"Xander *is* incredibly intense," Breena agrees while sitting perfectly still. "He always has been, even when he was a kid. But I have to say, it's been so fun seeing him smile more since the two of you seem to be working through the worst of your past."

"He didn't smile for a long time," Lucy agrees. The words are a hit, right to the heart.

"I know I hurt him." I swallow and then sigh as I gather a new piece of hair to curl.

"Please don't get mad when I say this," Lucy says as she brushes foundation onto her cheeks. "You didn't just hurt him. You *destroyed* that man. It was really sad. And for a long time, I just didn't get it. I didn't understand what could have happened between you two to cause that kind of reaction from you. Of course, now we know, and I understand it was just as devastating for you. So, it makes me happy to see that you're moving forward together."

"I don't *ever* want to repeat that, and I guess it's good to know that I won't have to."

"I hope you don't," Breena agrees.

"It won't happen again. I can't get pregnant. Whoa!"

Breena whirls around. She's lucky I'd just let go of a curl, or I would have burned her.

"What?" Lucy demands. "How do you know that?"

"The procedure didn't go well," I reply, licking my lips. "My uterus was pretty damaged. Pregnancy is highly unlikely to ever happen again. And, honestly, I think I'm okay with that. Sure, I wanted children, but I just don't think it's in the cards for me, and I can live with that. You'll both have a dozen babies each for me to spoil. It's fine."

Breena tilts her head to the side. "It's fine."

"Sure."

"Oh, honey." Lucy crosses to me, brush still in hand, and hugs me. "It's not fine, but everything will be okay."

"I know." I'm shocked that tears don't even threaten. "I know it will be okay. Now, turn back here, Breen, so I can finish your hair and then start on mine. We have to leave in an hour."

It takes me exactly that long to finish Breena's hair, tackle my own, and then put my makeup on.

But by the time we're all done and standing in front of a big, full-length mirror, I do believe it's been well worth the effort.

"We're hot," Lucy decides, taking stock of us.

"Superhot," Breena agrees.

I nod, looking us up and down with a critical eye.

Lucy is in a green, flowy gown that's just to die for. Breena's gown is purple and is perfect for her light blonde hair and fair complexion.

And my dress is *red*. Flowy like Lucy's, but mine has long bell sleeves and pretty embroidery around the hemline. I'm wearing a gold cuff bracelet my mother gave me years ago, along with a black tourmaline necklace.

"The guys might swallow their tongues." I grin in satisfaction just as the doorbell rings. "And here they are."

With our small clutch bags in hand, we make our way downstairs, and Breena opens the door.

Jonas and Giles wait on the other side, and Breena immediately laughs.

"Uh, babe? You live here. You don't have to ring the bell."

"I wanted to make sure it was safe before we just barged in," he replies.

I'm happy to hang back and watch both men take in the gorgeous sight of their girls. Their eyes sweep up and down, and the smiles that form on their lips are pure happiness and lust.

It's really pretty great.

Suddenly, I see Xander hurrying up the walk. Once he climbs the steps and sees me in the foyer, he stops dead in his tracks. He doesn't grin. His black-as-night eyes narrow, his jaw firms, and, sticking a finger in the air, he twirls it, instructing me to turn in a circle.

I quirk an eyebrow but do as he asks, rotating in a very slow, very deliberate circle.

When I meet his gaze once more, those smoldering eyes are intense as he says, "I'll be heading to jail tonight."

I smirk and walk to him, dragging my hand down his black lapel. "You look so handsome in a suit. It makes your shoulders look even broader than they are, which is saying a lot."

"All three of you look sharp," Lucy agrees. "I'd say we all clean up nicely."

"I've never been to a ball," Jonas admits as we walk down to the waiting cars. We have to take two vehicles tonight. "What, exactly, do we do there?"

"We dance," Lucy replies, then laughs at his horrified expression. "Drink bad punch. Socialize. Check out everyone else's pretty clothes."

"It's pretty much horrible," Giles adds, slapping Jonas on the shoulder. "But it's just one night."

"It's not *awful*," Breena says with a laugh. "It can be fun."

"I don't think I've ever heard a man refer to the ball as *fun*," Xander adds, sticking to Giles's side. "But we'll tolerate it. For you."

"How chivalrous of you," I reply before we climb into our vehicles and head out. They're holding the ball at the old town hall. We won't be able to drive all the way there because the streets downtown have been closed to foot traffic, but we're able to get pretty close.

The walk wouldn't usually take long, except we get a lot of curious looks, and several tourists stop us to ask for a photo, so it takes a few minutes more than normal to get there.

Once inside, we immediately find out parents, who are huddled with some of the other members of our coven, laughing and telling stories.

I *love* seeing them all together in their gorgeous, flowy gowns. Of course, my mom and Hilda are both wearing witches' hats.

"Do you understand," Xander begins, his lips against my ear as his hand rubs up and down my hip, "how incredibly beautiful you are, Lorelei?"

I smile up at him, my heart almost bursting when I see the love in his eyes as he gazes down at me.

"I can't tell you how happy I am to hear that you think so."

"You'd bring the gods to their knees." He rubs his finger over the tourmaline at my neck. "Thank you for wearing this."

"Where's yours?"

He pulls a hand out of his pocket and opens it to reveal a big chunk of the stone in his palm.

"Thank *you*."

He nods as he places it back into his pocket.

For the first time in a *long* time, I can honestly say we have fun. We dance, we laugh, and we talk about things that have nothing at all to do with a curse or a killer.

We simply enjoy our community and our love for each other and *have fun*.

I didn't realize until tonight how badly I needed this. How badly we *all* needed it.

"I need to use the restroom," I inform my mother. The men are off chatting about something mechanical since Percy has decided to buy himself a new car. The ladies are spread out, mingling, but I wanted to hang close to my mom for a while.

Something—my guides, maybe?—told me to, so I have been.

But all seems well, and I can't wait to use the restroom any longer.

"We'll be right here, darling," Mom says with a grin. "Grab yourself a drink on your way back."

"I might just do that."

Friends who wish to compliment me on my gown or ask how my book is coming along stop me several times, and I don't mind delaying to chat for a moment here and there.

Finally, I make my way into a bathroom stall and sigh with relief.

I wash my hands, fix my hair, and apply a fresh coat of lipstick before returning to the party.

But when I walk out of the restroom, I stumble to a stop.

Do not react.

I suck in a deep breath and repeat the mantra, saying it over and over again as I look around the room. All the people, every person I love, is dead.

They're still standing, facing me, with empty white eyes and no expressions on their faces. Their skin has begun to decay, showing the muscle, ligaments, and bone underneath.

It's disgusting. Vile.

And terrifying.

But I will not give *it* even an ounce of delight at seeing me scared.

"You hold no power here." My voice is low but strong. "You are not welcome. I banish you from this place, from these walls. Only love and light may stay. I call on my element, my guides, and my ancestors to help me in clearing this unwanted pest."

I blink, and the room is magically right again. People dressed in beautiful outfits dance and laugh. It's obvious that only I saw what just happened.

And although it was damn horrible, I'm glad that it was only for me and that it didn't ruin everyone else's evening.

"You're done ruining things for us," I mutter as I make my way back to my mother.

"There you are. I was about to send out a search party."

"I wasn't gone long."

"At least an hour," she says with a concerned frown. "Are you okay, darling?"

"I think so." Did *it* have me in some kind of a trance for almost an hour? I know I stopped to chat with friends, but that was only for a minute or two here and there. It certainly didn't take me that long to use the restroom.

My eyes scan the room until I find Xander, who's listening to Percy talk to the group of guys.

Suddenly, he turns his head and pins me with his gaze. As if *I need you* is written across my forehead, he excuses himself from the others and makes his way to me.

I take his proffered hand, and he pulls me out onto the dance floor. Tugging me into his arms, we sway back and forth to a slow song.

"What happened?" he asks me quietly.

"It's nothing to get upset over. I'll tell you about it later. For now, I just want to stand here in your arms, swaying to this music. We never danced enough. You're surprisingly good at it."

"We'll dance more," he promises and kisses the top of my head. Sometimes, I wonder if it looks weird, how he's so much taller than me, and I'm so petite next to him. Especially during moments like these, when we're dancing, and the size difference is so obvious.

But really, at the heart of it, I just don't care.

I think we fit together perfectly.

"That was so much fun." I grin over at Xander as he drives us through the residential part of Salem toward my cottage. "I think we all needed it."

"We did," he confirms, checking the rearview mirror. "It was nice to forget about things and just enjoy one another for the night."

"That's exactly what I thought." I reach over and grab his hand, giving it a squeeze. "My dress was even comfortable, which is a huge bonus."

"Your dress should be illegal in all fifty states. All I could think about was getting you out of it and seeing it in a ball by the side of my bed."

"Reeeeally." I know my smile is one of pure satisfied female. "Well then, my job here is done for the day."

That makes him snicker, and then he pulls my hand up to his lips, kisses my knuckles, and glances my way with a satisfied grin of his own.

Just that simple gesture makes my core muscles tighten in anticipation.

"Sex with you is fun." I don't know why I suddenly blurted that out, but I decide to go with it. "I mean, sure, I don't have much to compare it to, but it's a damn good time. Add on to that all the foreplay, flirting, and touches, and well...yeah. It's good stuff."

He doesn't say anything for a long minute, just holds my hand as he drives us to my house, so I finally look over at him.

His face is completely sober and still.

"Xander?"

"Hold on," he says. "I'm thinking of giraffes and Mexican food so I don't give in to the urge to pull this car over and fuck you on the side of the road."

I laugh in relief. "You scared me. I thought you were suddenly possessed or something."

"Nope, just trying to keep it together over here. You can't just say shit like that to me and not expect me to need to be inside of you, Lorelei."

"I was just thinking out loud, that's all."

But I do love the way his jaw clenches and his hands fist over the wheel, making his knuckles turn white.

Knowing that I can do that to this strong and powerful witch is damn satisfying.

"What are you thinking now?" he asks, but then quickly shakes his head. "Never mind. Don't tell me. I don't really want to know."

"The girls and I were talking today about how you and I can't read each other's minds," I tell him, shifting in the seat so I'm facing him. "I know that Jonas and Lucy cast the spell that makes them able to do that, but I told them I liked knowing we can't read each other's thoughts. I like surprising you and being surprised *by* you. How do you feel about it?"

He nods slowly, obviously thinking it over. He pulls into my driveway and cuts the engine, but neither of us moves to get out of the car.

We always used to love to talk in the car in the dark.

"Like you, I enjoy the mystery. I can read most people's minds. Not all, and I never break trust by poking my brain in where it's not wanted."

"I know you don't."

"But yeah, I can see a lot, and I think that's one of the things I've always loved about being with you—that I can't see inside your head. It makes me feel like we're just a normal couple, and it's something I don't want to change."

"I couldn't agree more."

"However..." He takes my hand again and kisses my fingertips, then presses my palm to his chest. "I have thought about suggesting that we link ourselves together until this mess is all over. I don't like the idea of not being able to connect with you in the event something goes sideways. Like at Beltane. If we'd been linked—"

"I don't know that it would have changed anything. You can't beat yourself up about that, Xander."

"I almost lost you." It's a whisper, one filled with regret and pain and fear. "I almost lost you at my own hands, and if that had happened, I wouldn't have been able to forgive myself."

"Whoa." I shift over to him and straddle his lap, the steering wheel digging into my back, although I don't really care. "You need to stop that, right here and now. First of all, *you* didn't do anything to hurt me. That was something completely out of your control. Secondly, I don't disagree. I have given it the same thought, being linked until this is over and then going back to normal might be good."

"Maybe we should." He drags his fingers down my cheek gently. I tip my forehead to his and wrap my arms around his neck, seeking as much comfort as I'm offering. "Maybe we should do that tomorrow. It'll be weird, and it might feel invasive, but we can either turn it right back off or break the connection once our quest is over."

"Tomorrow," I agree and then kiss him softly. "Please, my love, stop beating yourself up for something you didn't do. You're so strong and powerful, and I know in my heart of hearts that you would *never* harm me, whether we're together or not. What happened isn't your fault."

He sighs and then tugs my shoulders back so he can look into my eyes.

"I've needed to hear you say exactly those words for almost three years. For very different reasons."

Now the tears *do* prick the backs of my eyes. "I know. I know you did, and I'm sorry I couldn't give them to you. But I do mean them, Xander. For everything. What happened three years ago, at Beltane, everything."

"Thank you." He crushes me against him and holds on so tightly it's a wonder I can breathe.

Not that I mind.

Finally, after a few moments like that, I gently push away. "We should check things out. And I want to grab my altar to bring with me. It won't take long, and then we can go to your house and get mushy some more."

"Let's do it."

He helps me off his lap, and we slide out of the car. The front door is still locked, and when I walk inside, I see that Xander's right.

Everything is as I left it.

I take a deep breath and close my eyes, reaching out with my mind and searching for anything that might be wrong energetically.

But every corner of the house is clean.

"It's all good. You were right."

"I'm glad." He kisses my head. "Go pack up your things. I'm going back to the bedroom to pack up the last of the things I have here. I might as well take them home and wash them. I can bring them back."

"Good idea."

With a nod, he walks down the hall to the bedroom, and I turn to grab a box from the hall closet, when suddenly, I hear the music.

And it's more beautiful than ever.

CHAPTER SEVENTEEN
XANDER

Half of the clothes are clean, and half are dirty, so I toss them all into the hamper because I'll just wind up washing them all together.

It's easiest.

I have no idea how I ended up leaving so much here in such a short time.

I realize that Lorelei didn't grab her pillow the other day, so I pick that up, along with the baby blanket under it.

She'll want these.

After I skim the area to quickly assess if we should take anything else with us for now, I carry the hamper out to the living area.

"I think I have everything from back there. I didn't realize you didn't take your pillow and the blanket, so I grabbed that, too."

I glance around but quickly realize that I'm alone in the house.

And the front door is standing open.

"Lora!" Just to be sure, I quickly run through the other rooms of the small house and then straight out the front door. My heart is hammering, the blood in my ears rushing, and I absolutely *refuse* to let my mind torment me with the possibilities of what's happening.

For all I know, she just took some stuff out to the car.

But deep down, I know that's not the case.

I make myself stop to scan the area. It's dark, but I can see the shoreline, the cliffs down that shoreline, and then I see Lorelei standing at the top of those cliffs, her dress billowing in the wind around her. My heart falters.

Immediately, I shift into my wolf form and run down the sand at top speed, not caring at all that the sharp rocks tear at my feet. My only concern is getting to her. *Fast.*

When I'm roughly twenty feet away, I slow and shift back into the man so I can pull her out of the trance I can see she's in.

"Lorelei."

She turns to look back at me, her dress continuing to flow around her, the waves crashing up high. On any other day, this would be a gorgeous photo.

Today, it's terrifying.

"Snap out of it, baby."

Unfortunately, she ignores me and turns back to the water. She steps forward as if to throw herself over the side, and I rush at her, wrap my arms around her, and pull her back to safety.

She's crying. Not wailing, screaming cries, but silent tears that roll down her cheeks.

"Let me go," she says. "It's so beautiful. I want to go."

"No." I turn her to me and shake her shoulders roughly. "Listen to me. Look at me, Lorelei."

But her stare is empty.

I've never felt as useless as I have these past few weeks. First, her car accident, and now this.

"Lorelei. Love. Heart of my heart." I make myself calm down and rest my forehead against hers. She immediately calms, but we're not out of the woods yet. "Please. Come back to me now. Don't let *it* have the satisfaction of seeing you like this. You're the strongest person I know, Lorelei. Come on."

She sighs, grips my waist, and I know she's back. It's as if a switch has been flipped.

"Xander?"

"I'm taking you home." Grimly, I pick her up and carry her back to the cottage. "What do you need to take with you? Were you able to gather anything?"

"I—" She shakes her head. "My altar. Some stones and shells."

"Let's get them. Because we're not coming back here until this is all over."

"I can walk."

I set her down and am so fucking proud of her when

she raises her chin and walks into her house, slamming the door behind us.

"I'm so sick of this shit," she mutters as she starts to fill a box with her things. I notice her fingers are shaking, but I don't comment on it.

She needs to get through the next ten minutes. Then, once I get her home, she can fall apart.

"I want this terrarium," she says, passing it to me. "And these shells. Oh, I need a couple of books."

She hustles back to her office and returns with much more than a *couple* of books. I take them from her.

"I have my grandmother's grimoire there. I should have taken it before."

"We have it now," I assure her. "What else?"

"Well, we can't just pack up the whole house, so this should do it for now. If I need something else, I'll just buy it."

"Fine by me, I'll buy you whatever you want. Let's get the fuck out of here."

She won't stop pacing. We've only been home for fifteen minutes, but she's spent that whole time pacing around my living room, moving into the library and then back out again, that dress and her auburn hair flowing around her in a dramatic scene fit for a movie.

She's magnificent.

And she worries me.

Finally, before I can say anything, she starts to tug at her dress, trying to get out of it.

"I can't breathe in this thing," she says as she pulls at the material. "Help me, please."

She's almost frantic, as if she's having a panic attack, and I don't like it. I help her out of the dress. She unfastens the strapless bra and tosses it aside, too, and then, with just her underwear on, she runs up the stairs with me hot on her heels.

There's no way I'm leaving her alone right now.

She pulls a simple T-shirt over her head, steps into some sweats, and then ties her hair up in a bun, sighing in relief.

"That's better." Then she turns to me. "Sorry, this isn't the sexy scene I was hoping for."

"I'm worried about you."

She pauses, frowns, and then walks back to me to take my hand. "Let's go back downstairs, okay?"

"We can go wherever you want."

She leads me to the living room and sits on the couch. But then she pops up again and returns to pacing.

"I'm just so *mad*," she finally says. "It got in my house. In my *home*. Despite the fact that I have wards and sigils and crystals in a grid around it, it got to me there, and that just pisses me off."

"Understood." I sit and watch her pace, full of angry energy.

"Is it because I left the door open while we went about gathering things?"

"That could be. We left an opening unattended, and that's how it slithered its way inside to you."

"In. My. House. I swore after Beltane that it wouldn't get to me there ever again. Because I can't be like Breena, Xander. I can't leave my home the way she did. I know it worked out for her in the end because of Giles, but I can't do that. I like your place. It's really nice, and I like being here, but my cottage comes from my mom. And *her* mom. And it's by the water, and you know how I need that."

"I know." I also know that I'll be moving in with her and selling this house or renting it out in the future. She needs that place, and I need her, so it's a no-brainer.

"And now it fucked with me there and tainted it for me. And I'm just so mad. I refuse to be afraid in my own home."

"Okay, at the risk of having you slap me, I'm going to tell you to take a deep breath. Take a breath, baby."

She does as I ask. She plants her feet, closes her eyes, and pulls in a long, deep breath.

When she opens her eyes again, she frowns at me. "I'm still pissed."

"I know, but I need you to calm down a little because we're not resolving anything this way."

"I'd rather be worked up than afraid," she admits, but she does sit at the other end of the couch, then pulls her feet up under her and faces me.

"Do you feel sick?"

The anger clears from her face and makes way for surprise. "Actually, no. I don't. And I didn't, even right after when you carried me home. That was nice, by the way."

She takes another deep breath, and I see some of the anger leave her, her shoulders falling just a little bit.

"It honestly wouldn't have fucked with me so badly if it hadn't gotten to me inside my house. Outside is one thing, but that's my sanctuary."

"Totally understandable, of course. How did you get out to the cliffs so fast?"

She blinks and then frowns. "The cliffs?"

"Yeah. I was only in the bedroom for about ten minutes. By the time I came out and realized you were gone, you were at the top of the cliffs. That's at least a twenty-minute walk."

"I have no idea." She nibbles on her thumbnail, trying to remember. "Holy shit, I don't know."

"Okay, we're not going to focus on that right now. I think we should get some rest. It's past midnight."

"I don't know if I can sleep." The admission is a whisper. I reach over and pull her to me, done with not touching her. We both need the connection. "I don't want to dream."

"I'm right here." The hamper is close by, so I reach in and snag the baby blanket, pressing it to her heart. "We're right here."

"You brought it."

"I couldn't believe you forgot it."

"I didn't." She sniffs the blanket and then spreads it out over both of us. "I thought it might help protect the house. Silly, I know, but I also know that you wove a protection spell into this before you gave it to me. I figured it couldn't hurt."

"How did you know about the spell?"

"I know *you*. It's something you would do for us." She leans in closer and rests her head on my chest. "I'm going to sound like a whiner for a minute. I'm warning you."

"Go for it."

"I don't want to do this anymore." She turns sad eyes up to mine, and my heart immediately aches for her. "I don't want to, Xander. It's scary and unnerving, and I want it to be done."

"We're so close." I rest my lips on her forehead and kiss her lightly. "Almost there, sweetheart. And then we can put everything behind us and just live our lives."

"I want that. More than you can possibly know. What happens to us when it's all done?"

"What do you mean?"

"Between you and me. *Us.*"

"We're together. Always. The way it's supposed to be. Do you think I'm simply hooking up with you now as a distraction, and we wouldn't be together later?"

"No." She laughs a little and shakes her head. "I guess I just needed the reassurance, that's all."

"You're stuck with me forever. You're mine in all life-times and all the time in between."

"And you're mine." She lazily drags her fingers up and down my forearm. "And it doesn't bother you that we can't have more babies?"

That's a sting in the heart. It always will be because Lorelei would be an amazing mother.

"You are my family, Lorelei. Whether we have a dozen kids or none at all, that doesn't change."

"That was the right answer."

I feel her getting heavier against me. "Baby, you're *so* tired. We should go up and go to sleep."

"Can we stay here?"

"Are you afraid of the bedroom?"

"No." Her voice is soft. "No, I just want to be here by the door in case *it* tries to get in."

I hug her close and flick my fingers to dim the lights. "We can stay here. You sleep. I'll hold you. I'm right here, baby. Nothing's going to hurt you while I've got you."

"I know." Her sigh is both weary and relieved as she drifts off to sleep, clutching both me and the blanket in her small yet strong hands.

The truth is, I share her anger. I would like nothing more in the universe than to get my hands around *its* neck and choke the life out of it.

If it were human, that is.

But it's not, so I have to find other ways to make it suffer.

Because it won't simply die. No. It'll die in pain,

anguish, and in perpetual torment for all it's done to Salem and the people I love.

I *know that I'm dreaming. I always know, whether it's a fun dream or a nightmare. Sometimes, it's me astral projecting to a different timeline or a different universe altogether. Traveling has almost become a hobby of mine.*

I'm not a stranger to such things, and I've learned to control it.

But this time is different.

I'm packing the hamper in Lorelei's bedroom, gathering my clothes, the blanket, Lora's pillow, and the other small things to bring with me.

Then, I stop by the office to gather some books for her, knowing she'll want them. The hamper is heavy by the time I reach the living room, where the front door is standing open.

But Lorelei isn't gone.

She's standing before me, soaked from head to toe, including the dress, which has to weigh fifty pounds with all the water. Her hair is drenched.

It's as though she took a swim in the ocean.

But her eyes...they're not white.

They're black.

She opens her mouth, and water flows out of it before she starts to speak to me.

"We've lost. I'm dead, just like Agatha and all the others. All dead. It's going to kill you, too."

"No, this is a dream."

She smiles in a horrible distortion of what her actual smile is like. "Only a dream of what's to come. You can't stop it. I controlled you once, and I can do it again. You think you're so strong. Everyone thinks you're strong, and they trust you, but you'll let them all down again. Because I'm the strong one. I hold the kind of power you can only wish for."

I laugh, and Lorelei opens her mouth and screams.

"Hey." My eyes flutter open, and Lorelei pats my cheek soothingly, her sweet face frowning up at me. "You're just having a dream. It's okay."

I suck in a breath and then simply hug her close.

"Bad one," I murmur against her hair.

"That's unusual for you," she replies. She pushes her fingers through my hair, and it feels like magic. Because *she's* magic. "I was always the one with the bad dreams."

"I should have figured it would happen. I'm sorry, I need to get up for a second."

"Oh, of course." She easily moves off my lap, and I stand to get some water and pace the room a bit while my mind clears. "Wanna talk about it?"

"I do. Of course, I do." I pass her the water and then sit next to her once more. She doesn't climb into my lap, but she does rest her leg on mine, keeping our connection. "I meant to tell you earlier about what happened at the ball, but then we got preoccupied with other things."

"What happened?"

I swallow hard, remembering the moment in the ballroom when I thought the earth had fallen out from under me.

"I was standing there, talking with the guys, and I glanced around to find you. I like knowing where you are if you're not with me."

"I know." She grins, not seeming at all bothered by that comment, and takes a sip of the water. "Go on."

"When I looked around, I saw that everyone else was fine, going about their business, but you were hanging from a noose from the ceiling. Obviously, I was the only one who saw it because everyone else was just carrying on as if nothing at all was wrong. And, of course, I *knew* instantly that it wasn't real. It still gave me a jolt, but I understood I was being toyed with. Add that to seeing you on that cliff, and your intent to jump, and it's no wonder I had a nightmare."

"Okay, this has layers." She passes the water back to me. "First of all, I had a very similar experience at the ball. Except when I came out of the bathroom, *everyone* was dead. Zombies. Pretty gross. I also refused to react and said a little protection spell that seemed to piss *it* off enough to go away. But my mom said I'd been gone for an hour, and it felt like only minutes for me."

"I hate that asshole," I grumble.

"Oh, same goes. The second layer is, I can't believe I really would have jumped off that cliff tonight."

"Had I not been there, you absolutely would have."

She shakes her head stubbornly. "Xander, I hate heights. There's no way."

"*It* was controlling you. Of course, I don't believe you would have willingly thrown yourself off the cliff, but you didn't have a say in the matter. And it took a lot for me to bring you out of that trance. It's some creepy shit, Lorelei."

"What was the dream about?" she asks.

"You. At your house. But you were dead, from jumping off the cliffs. The fucked-up part?"

"Oh, there's an *actual* fucked-up part? Because I thought we were already there."

"Ha ha. The really fucked-up part was that it was using you to speak, so it was you talking, but it was really *it*. And I pissed it off because I laughed at it."

"Yeah, we're pretty bad for the ego, that's for sure. I'm sorry you saw that. We need to tell the others first thing in the morning."

"I agree, but it's interesting that *it* isn't really fucking with the others this time around. Seems to be focused on the two of us."

"Honestly, I'm okay with that." She bites her lip and leans her head back on the sofa. "If we're the target, that means it's leaving the others alone."

"That we're aware of."

Lorelei sighs. "Yeah, that we're aware of. Do you think that if we were linked psychically, we could pull each other out of the visions and dreams that aren't real? That we could protect each other?"

"I think it's worth a try," I reply immediately. "I'll go get the grimoire. Let's do it now and then go get in a real bed to get some decent sleep. We'll do a sleep spell for no nightmares and to protect our minds while we're unconscious."

"So much spell work lately," she mutters as she follows me into the library where the grimoire is waiting. "I went from *no* witch work to all the Craft in the land in a matter of minutes. I love it, but it can be a smidge overwhelming."

"I hate that you left the Craft behind when you went to California."

"I needed to." She shrugs a shoulder as I flip through the book to the page I need. "I needed the break. It was good for me. But that's done."

"Good, because we need your magic. *You* need it."

"And I have it. Okay, let's read each other's minds. Wait. Are you a pervert? Like, do you think about boobs and sex all the time?"

"Only *your* boobs and sex with you, so it should be okay."

She rolls her eyes, and it makes me laugh as I take her hand in mine. "Ready?"

"Ready. I'll read it with you."

With harm to none, blessings to all, we cast this spell, this is our call.

Across time and space, our minds become one, tethered together under moon as in sun.

Your thoughts will be mine, my dreams become yours,
within arm's reach as on distant shores.

Choices remain, for me and for thee,

As I will it, so mote it be.

Hello? Are you there?

I grin down at her. I can hear her voice in my head as plainly as if she's speaking aloud.

I'm here. Can you hear me now?

She laughs, clearly delighted. "So weird. But kind of fun. Now, I'm totally exhausted. Let's go upstairs and get some sleep."

"I'm all for that."

I return the grimoire to its place, and then with Lorelei's hand in mine, I lead her up the stairs to the bedroom.

I can hear her thoughts.

I'm so tired. Why does he have such a good butt? This is a lot of stairs. I need to work out more.

"I'm tired, too. I'm glad you like my butt, and I think you're in fine shape."

Lorelei laughs again. "Yep, you can hear me. I'll have to watch what I think. Though I have no idea how to do that."

"We'll figure it out."

Chapter Eighteen
Lorelei

This has been the most productive week I've had in over a year. Things have seemed normal all week since the night of the ball. There have been no scary things jumping out, no music putting me in a suicidal trance, and without tempting fate, I could almost say we're just a couple of normal people living our lives.

Witchy lives, sure, and I can read my man's thoughts, but all in all, it's been pretty mundane.

I even wrote more than a quarter of my book this week. With most of my research done, the words just poured out of me, and I found myself at the computer more than I was away from it. It felt great.

But all the quiet makes me nervous because Samhain is just a week away, and I know we're about to have a shitstorm on our hands.

At least, we've had a week to rest and recharge.

With more than half of a chapter already written for the day, I carry my empty coffee mug into the kitchen to get a refill. Xander returned from flying over Salem just a little while ago and is currently reading in the library.

So, I fix him a cup of coffee, as well, then carry both mugs into the library, where I find him hunched over an open book on the table before him.

"I didn't know if you'd want it, but I made you some coffee." I set the mug at his elbow and look over his shoulder to see what his reading material is. "Are you reading about *vampires*?"

"Yeah." He reaches for the coffee and smiles up at me. "Thanks for the coffee."

"Do you suspect that vampires are holding Hallows End hostage?"

His lips turn up in a slight smile, and it sends tingles down my spine. For the love of Freya, the man is beautiful.

"I kind of love that you think about how attracted you are to me so often," he says casually. "But you're going to give me a big head."

"Yeah, yeah." I can't help but laugh and kiss his cheek. "You know you're hot. What's up with the vampires?"

"I needed a palate cleanser." He shrugs a shoulder and watches me over the rim of his mug. "How's the writing?"

"It's been going really well. I'm almost done for the day already. I have to tell you, now that we can see what the other sees, along with knowing our thoughts, it's *so cool* when you're the raven. No wonder you love shifting into it so often. It's exhilarating."

He tips his head to the side, watching me. "It hadn't occurred to me that you'd be able to see that. I'm glad you can because it's not something I can really put into words."

"I can see that. Also, the process of actually shifting is so weird. I guess I always thought it would hurt, but it doesn't."

"If it hurt, I wouldn't do it very often."

"Makes sense. Do you notice anything that I do that surprises you?"

"Your thoughts are fascinating. You carry a lot of anxiety you don't voice, and that's something we'll have to talk about sometime because I want you to talk to me about that stuff. And you have one hell of an imagination."

"Always have." I wink at him and head for the door. "I'm going to go finish writing while I'm in the groove. Breena texted me. She wants us all to meet at the aunts' house later. Does that work for you?"

"It does. Just let me know when you'd like to go over."

"Okay." I turn to him, but he's already reabsorbed in the story he was reading. I know I could open myself up and see the words he's reading if I wanted to, but that's incredibly distracting. And if I did that, I wouldn't get anything else done. It's been a week of figuring out this psychic thing between us, but I think we have it down now.

I don't hate it. I might even suggest that we keep it open after we've finished our mission.

To my surprise, the next couple of hours go by quickly, and when I've finished with the chapter I wanted to see through today, Xander's waiting for me with an orange and a bottle of water.

"You need a snack."

"You're handy to have around." I accept the water and then lean in to kiss him. "We should go join the others. I think everyone else is already there."

"I was just waiting for you to finish," he replies with a nod.

The trip over to the aunts' house from Xander's doesn't take long, and when we pull into the driveway, I see that I was right. We're the last to arrive.

When we join the others in the kitchen, where we always congregate whenever we go to the aunts' house, it's full of laughter, noise, and the smell of cookies. Aunt Hilda always has cookies on hand.

Today, they smell like lemon.

"Hi, everyone!"

"Thank the goddess you're here," Breena says excitedly before running over to me. She throws her arms around my neck and hugs me close.

"What happened?" With panic making my heart beat double-time, I grip her shoulders and hold her steady. "Oh, goddess, what happened?"

"Nothing," Breena assures me. "Nothing bad. I'm sorry, I'm just so excited I had to hug you."

"Okay." I take a deep, relieved breath and will my heart to settle down. "Okay, good. I like good surprises. They're just few and far between these days. Have you been waiting for us to spill the beans?"

"Yes, and it's killing me," Lucy replies, chewing on a cookie.

I glance around the room and see that everyone's here. Mom, Hilda, and all six of us. Even Agatha is hovering in the corner, waiting to hear the news.

"Okay." Breena clasps her hands at her waist and grins like a maniac.

A good maniac.

"Just say it, child," my mom says, waving her hand as if to tell her to get on with it.

"I finished the tapestry of fate." Breena bounces on the balls of her feet, clapping her hands. "I'm *done.*"

"Good job, darling," Hilda says and hugs her daughter close. "That must be a relief. I know it's been such a struggle."

"Yeah, I'm over it," Breena admits. "Don't get me wrong, I was happy to do it for what we need it for, but it was so much work, and so much pressure. I'm relieved to have it finished."

"Do we get to see it?" Xander asks her.

"Of course. Giles?"

"That's my cue," Giles says and steps out the back

door. He's back seconds later with a large piece of card-board. It has to be four feet long by three feet wide.

When Breena pulls the sheet covering it away, we all gasp.

"Oh, Breena," I breathe.

We all gather close to examine it. The image is of a place I've only seen once before in the vision I had where I saw Hallows End.

There are buildings in that old Puritan style on the sides, and a path or dirt road in the middle. In the very center of the scene is a large fire.

The sky is dark, but the moon is full, and she wove in beautiful stars. There are trees and flowers that she embellished with real moss and beads and shells the rest of us gathered and put spells on for her.

"Every stitch has been so carefully crafted," Jonas murmurs, his eyes pinned to the artwork. "Breena, this is absolutely wonderful. Aside from the magic of it, and what we hope to use it for, it's a stunning piece of art. You're very talented."

"Thank you." Breena preens happily as we each take a turn pointing out something we especially love.

"I'm so proud of you." I wrap my arm around my cousin's shoulders and kiss her square on the cheek. "So freaking proud, Breen."

"I can feel the magic pulsing off this," Lucy adds as her hands hover six inches away from the stitching. "It's incredibly powerful."

"And that was the point," Xander reminds her.

"Because yes, it's beautiful. But the power it wields is intense. It's our best chance of breaking the curse."

"Thank you," Jonas says and kisses Breena's forehead. "Thank you for this gift, sweetheart."

"You're welcome."

———

We decided that the six of us should reconvene at Xander's house to make some solid plans now that Breena finished the tapestry.

"We don't have to necessarily wait for Samhain now that we have the right tool," Giles points out. "I say we go right away and lift this thing."

"We still don't have the right words for the spell," I remind him. "Don't get me wrong, I'm all for getting this done as quickly as possible, but we're missing a key ingredient."

"Maybe there isn't a specific spell," Breena points out. "Maybe it's magic we have to weave ourselves."

"You could have a point," Xander replies, his eyes narrowed. "I'd like to take one more look through Katrina's Book of Shadows, just to be sure."

He lifts his hand, and the grimoire shoots out of the wall and lands in Xander's hand.

Show-off.

He glances over at me and gives me that killer smile.

If a man has a gift, he should use it.

Yeah, yeah.

Chuckling, he pages through the book.

"Stop," Breena says, holding out a hand. "Did you see those empty pages? There are a couple of blank ones toward the back."

Xander finds what Breena's talking about and shrugs. "They're just empty. Maybe they were stuck together or something, so she simply skipped them."

"Would she do that, Jonas?" I ask. "She was your sister, you should know."

"She may have. Or she knew she wanted to come back to add something there later and never got around to it."

"Hmm." I tap my lip with my finger and then decide to stand and grab a slice of pizza that we ordered earlier.

But in doing that, I knock over my water, and it splashes on the grimoire.

"Shit, I'm sorry."

Before I can reach over to wipe the water away, Xander holds up a hand.

"Wait."

"I don't want the water to soak through—"

"Just wait," Xander says again. "Something's happening."

I blink, shocked to see words appearing on the page where the water hit the paper.

"More water," Lucy says, reaching for the glass.

"Hold on, we don't want to ruin the rest of the book," Breena adds and quickly works to protect the other pages from getting wet. "Okay. But paint the water on slowly. Just enough to dampen but not soak it."

"Thank the gods you're here to keep a level head because I would have just poured," I say with a chuckle. I dip my finger into the water and gently begin moistening the page.

As I do, more words magically appear.

"She used the magical ink," Jonas whispers with excitement. "We made it when we were teenagers. And it worked."

"There's a letter," Giles says.

"It's addressed to you, Jonas." Breena points at the page and then pats Jonas's arm. "Read it."

Dearest Brother,

I do not know how much time I have. You plan to cast the curse soon, and I suspect it will be this night, during the full moon of Samhain.

I wish I could have convinced you to forget the notion of the curse. I understand that you are afraid for your people, as we have only begun in this ridiculous hysteria, but you do not understand the consequences of your actions.

I know that as soon as you cast the curse, I will forget you. It will be as though you never were, and that rips at my heart, for I love you, precious brother. I do not know what my life will be without you.

All I can do is hope and pray to all the gods and goddesses that this ink works, and that I can write the lifting spell in this book before you finish your ritual. I pray I am in time.

Please know, I have loved you all your life. From the moment you were born until I take my last breath, I will love you. You have been a treasure in my life.

Your sister,

Katrina

"Well, damn." I wipe tears from my cheeks and see that there isn't a dry eye in the place.

"The next page," Giles says. "Was she able to write the lifting spell?"

Jonas turns the page, and I see that it's blank, so I again carefully paint a very light layer of water onto the paper, and more words appear.

"It's here," Xander says. "It's all here."

Lucy begins reading the words, but suddenly, Breena joins her.

And she's not looking at the book.

With my eyes narrowed on her, I cock my head to the side. "Breen? How do you know this spell?"

"I think I wrote it," she says slowly. "I know every word of it."

Xander's eyes narrow as he watches her. "Breena, you and Jonas have had a special bond since we met him."

"Yes," Jonas adds, also watching Breena carefully. "Could it be?"

"Are you thinking that Breena is Katrina reincarnated?" Giles asks.

"That's exactly what I think," Xander says. "I can do a past-life regression session with you right now if you're up for it."

Breena blinks, obviously overwhelmed. "Well, you're the one I trust the most with that sort of thing. So, yes. We need to know. *I* need to know. Because I've felt close to Jonas, and I *know* that spell. As soon as Lucy started saying the words, I just knew it."

"Would you be more comfortable lying down?" Xander asks her.

"Probably. Can we go to the living room?"

"We can do whatever you want," I assure her with a smile. "Let's get you comfortable and relaxed. We're not in a hurry, understand?"

"Sure. This is exciting. Jonas, what if I am your sister?"

"Not only would it explain a lot," he says, cupping Breena's cheek in his hand, "but it would be the best gift."

"Aww, that's sweet," Lucy says.

Once we get Breena settled on the couch, Xander lowers all the blinds in the room to make it dim and relaxing.

He sits next to Breena in a chair by the couch, and the rest of us all take a seat, mindful to be quiet so we don't interfere in any way.

"Okay, Breena, this is going to be fairly simple. It's not hypnosis as much as it is guided remembrance. I'm going to lead you through a meditation exercise and help you fully relax, and then we'll start the regression. How does that sound?"

"Really nice, actually. I could use some relaxation."

"Perfect." Xander smiles kindly at her and leans forward, his elbows on his knees. "Go ahead and close your pretty eyes. Take a deep breath, inhaling with my count of four. One, two, three, four. Good. Now exhale, also to a count of four."

He takes her through the breathing exercises and then begins the actual meditation.

"You're in a garden that I like to keep in my mind," Xander begins. "I'd like to share it with you today. There are many trees and plenty of shade, with places to sit and listen to the birds. I have friends here. Sometimes, a deer might walk through, or maybe a friendly dog. You're not too hot nor too cold, and you feel calm and happy to be here."

Breena takes another deep breath as if she's settling into being in the garden.

"Now, we're going to walk down a path. It's a pleasant day, and you're not afraid. The path winds through some trees and leads you to a small creek that rolls gently by. The water is warm, and you decide to lie in it so it washes over you from the head down. You're floating in that wonderful creek, and you can see that when you lift your hand out of it, it's not wet. If you were to stand and get out, you would be as dry as you were before you lay down."

Breena's breathing has evened out, and I can see she's completely relaxed while listing to the deep timbre of Xander's voice.

"I'm going to walk you back in time as you let that

water move over you. It's washing away all the junk you've carried with you. All the stress and worry, and any fear or sadness. It's washing down the creek, leaving you worry-free. I want you to think back to when you were a child playing with Lorelei and Lucy in your mother's backyard. Making your special quilt."

My eyes narrow. I don't remember telling him about the quilt.

"Now, we're going back further. As far as you want to go. I want you to invite your guides, your ancestors, and your higher self to walk with you now. To protect you and guide you back from this lifetime to others. You're safe, you're loved, and you're protected as we go on this journey. You're going to step out of that creek now, fully dry and free of any of the worry you've carried with you in this life, and together with your guides, you're going to get back on the path and walk back in time as we know it."

I can't help but press my lips together. I knew Xander was gifted, but watching him do this is amazing. So soothing and loving.

"Have you been walking?" he asks Breena.

Her eyes are moving back and forth behind her eyelids, and she parts her lips to respond.

"Yes," she says. Her voice is soft and dreamy.

"What do you see?"

"I'm a man."

"Can you tell *when* this is?"

She pauses, her brows furrowing into a frown.

"There are really old cars on the road. Cobblestones. I see ships in the harbor. It looks like Salem. I need to get home to my children."

"Good. Excellent. Now, I want you to ask your guides to take you farther down the path. Keep going back."

He walks her through two more lifetimes. In one, she's a child who seems to be dying from tuberculosis. In the other, she's a widowed mother who makes ends meet by sewing.

"Okay, let's keep walking farther," Xander urges. "There's no rush."

Behind the blinds, I can see that the sun has set. They've been working for more than two hours. Several times, one of us has gotten up to go to the restroom or fetch water for everyone, but no one wants to leave for long because it's too fascinating.

"I'm a woman," Breena says. "I'm definitely a witch. Powerful. I'm married, and some of my children have died."

Jonas sits up, clearly knowing what Breena's talking about.

"Oh, it's horrible. So much fear. I don't understand why innocent people are being captured and killed. The people they're killing aren't even witches. But some of them are my friends. Giles Corey was my friend. And, yes, he was a witch, but he was harmless."

"Katrina?" Jonas asks, speaking for the first time.

Xander doesn't tell him to stop talking, so he moves closer to Breena. "Are you Katrina?"

"Yes," she says. "I'm Katrina."

"Who is your mother?" Xander asks her.

"Marjorie," she replies, and Jonas nods. "And I have a sister."

"Do you have a brother?" Jonas asks.

"No." She shakes her head, but then she frowns. "Wait. Yes. Yes, I have a brother. *Before*, I had a brother. But then—now—I don't. I somehow forgot him."

Lucy wipes at a tear. Giles is riveted.

And Jonas reaches for her hand.

"I'm here," Jonas says. "I'm your brother, and I'm right here."

"There is so much chaos, and I want to tell Jonas to be patient. He's a good leader, a strong man. But he can be so impatient. I fear he won't listen to me. So, I write everything I can think of in my grimoire. In secret. No one can see."

"Thank you," Jonas says. "Thank you for writing it down."

"I do not know if he will ever see it. I am afraid, and we must flee to Boston."

It's interesting to me how her way of speaking has changed, as though she really is in 1692.

"We don't want you to be afraid," Xander says calmly. "There's no need to be scared now. Nothing can hurt you. We're going to start walking back. Are you ready to come back, Breena?"

"Yes." Her voice sounds normal again, and Xander proceeds to guide her back to the present time.

"When I tell you to open your eyes, you'll be calm and relaxed and will remember everything we talked about. Open your eyes, Breena."

Her eyes flutter open, and she looks around the room. Her gaze zeroes in on Jonas, and then she immediately launches herself into his arms, hugging him tightly.

"You're my *brother*."

"It explains so much," he says again. "Thank you for doing this."

"Are you kidding? It's so cool. But, you guys, there's no time to talk about past lives now. I know what we have to do to lift the curse of the blood moon."

CHAPTER NINETEEN

He is resting. Feeding on the energy of the water, letting his strength build so he can finish it all soon. So he can move on to what he needs.

So he can finally free himself.

He's always known that it would one day lead to this. It took far longer than it should have, and that angers him. But he sees the end now, and it's more beautiful than he could have ever imagined.

It's all about to end.

CHAPTER TWENTY
XANDER

"What do we have to do?" Lorelei demands as Breena stands and accepts the water Lucy offers her, then takes a soothing sip.

"We have to take the entire coven into Hallows End and speak the spell Katrina wrote in the grimoire."

"How do we get the whole coven over the bridge?" Giles demands as he pulls his wife into his arms and hugs her close. "Also, sidebar, that kind of scared the shit out of me. Let's not do it again, okay?"

"I was safe," Breena assures him and pats his cheek. "I promise. Xander would never put me at risk. You know that. He's your best friend."

"And he's the only one I'd trust with you like that. It still made me uneasy. So, before you go about saving the world here, I need you to take a deep breath, sweetheart."

They're sweet together, Lorelei says in my mind as Jonas reaches for his wife and tucks her against his side. *They're all so good together.*

We're all good together. I glance down at her and smile softly. *Marry me, Lorelei. When all of this is over, and we can move on with our lives as normally as possible, do me the honor of being my wife.*

Her eyes go round as she gazes up at me. I like that all six of us are taking a moment to center ourselves with the one who calms us the most.

I know it's not the most romantic time and place, but damn it, I love you so much. You are *love for me. You are my constant. Even when you were gone, I held on to knowing that you were safe and whole.*

We're better together than we are apart, she admits silently. *Why now? Why this moment?*

Because I know that I can't go through the rest of what we're about to go through if I have even one seed of doubt about the two of us. Because I want to know, deep in the marrow of my bones, that we're going to make it. That, on the other side of this, it's you and me.

She leans in closer and kisses my arm, then urges me down to kiss her on the lips.

"Of course, I'll marry you."

Lucy and Breena gasp as all eyes whip around to stare at us.

"It's about damn time," Lucy says smugly. "Also, could you redo that *not* telepathically so we can be in on how you proposed?"

I laugh and lift Lorelei into my arms, kissing her hard before setting her back on her feet.

"No."

"Damn."

"I would offer to run out and buy champagne to celebrate," Giles says, "but I think we have to finish this other thing before we can do an engagement celebration."

"Yeah, you're right." Lorelei sighs, but the grin on her face is one of pure happiness. "We'll party it up later. Then I have wedding plans to make."

"You have a week."

She spins and pins me with a shocked gaze. "What?"

"I want to get married on Samhain."

"*This* Samhain?" she demands. "Like, the one that falls in a week?"

"That's the one."

"Why the hurry?" Lucy asks. "Yes, I know, I got married in like four minutes, but seriously. Why the rush?"

"Because I'm done not having that permanent tie to you." I'm staring down into her gorgeous green eyes as I push her hair over her shoulder. "So, we can elope—"

"Oh, hell no," Lucy objects.

"—or you can plan a wedding in a week."

"I'll make it happen," Lorelei promises me. "I have everything we'll need anyway, and I also have some pretty amazing women in my life who can help with the details."

"I love this," Breena says with a soft, dreamy smile. "Okay, focus. We have a curse to lift, you guys."

"That's right," Giles says. "And my original question stands. How are we going to get the entire coven into Hallows End? And won't that freak everyone there out?"

"I suspect I can explain what's happening to everyone when we walk into town," Jonas says, tapping his chin as he thinks it over. "It might be odd to see a whole coven cross the bridge in the light of day, but—"

"Tonight," Breena says, shaking her head. "We're going *tonight*. We can make it happen."

"It's almost eleven now," Lorelei says. "Breena, our own coven will be sleeping, and we have to fill everyone in."

"It has to be tonight." Breena lifts her stubborn chin. "I know we can do this, you guys."

"I'm starting the phone tree," Lucy announces as she reaches for her phone. "I'll call the aunts first."

"We need crystals," Breena says, turning to Giles. "Big ones, not the small tumbleds."

"I have a lot of bigger geodes at the shop," Giles replies. "No problem."

"We have to incorporate the tapestry into this," Breena says, chewing her lip. "But I don't know *how*. It's flat. I don't know what to do with it."

"Why don't we mount it?" I suggest. "I can make a stake in the shape of the algiz rune, adding more protection, and mount the tapestry to that."

"Brilliant," Breena says excitedly. "Yes, that's perfect."

"The aunts are calling more people now," Lucy announces. "I told them to meet us by the gardens at my place. Since Hallows End is basically next to my property, that made sense to me."

"Good idea." I nod and take a deep breath. "Let's go solve this puzzle and lift a curse."

"Thank you all for coming so late." I raise my hand, making the nearby fire build higher so I can see my coven clearly. Suddenly, Jonas raises his hand, and twinkle lights begin mingling between everyone, lighting up the area like lightning bugs.

I turn to him and raise an eyebrow.

"You're not the only one with tricks," Jonas says with a grin. "This will help us see."

"Oh, this is pretty," Breena says, a happy smile on her face. "I want to learn this spell."

"I'll teach it to you," Jonas promises. "The way you taught it to me when I was a boy."

"Huh?" Mom blinks, obviously confused. "I think you need to catch us up on some things."

"I will. Don't worry. Anyway, as I was saying, thank you again for coming so quickly."

With hardly a moment's notice, everyone came to

Lucy's property right at the edge of the bridge that leads over to Hallows End.

"If you've figured out a way to lift that curse," Percy says, "we'll happily come and do everything we can to help. You know that."

"And I appreciate it."

"We all do," Jonas adds.

Not only did my coven family come, but they also came prepared, bringing their familiars, their tools, and wearing magical clothing.

They're ready for war.

I hope, with everything in me, that it doesn't lead to that, but it's good to know we're prepared if it does.

"We're all going into Hallows End," I inform them, filling them in on what we've just learned about Breena and Jonas this evening. "We found the spell to lift the curse, and the tapestry is finished. We have all the tools we need to lift this curse and free Hallows End."

"We need to join forces with Jonas's coven," Lorelei continues as she slips her hand in mine and holds on tightly. I can feel her magic flowing through her, and it bolsters mine. "Obviously, they won't understand at first, but Jonas is sure we can explain enough to them to convince them to help us."

"I do not believe we will have a problem with my people helping us," Jonas chimes in with a nod. "They are kind, and they *want* to help others. They'll be confused at first, but when it's all over, we will help them understand."

"I'm a counselor," one of our members chimes in. "I'll be happy to work with them if we need to."

"Me, too," someone else says.

"The tapestry of fate was woven to depict a moment in time when the curse has already been lifted, with the coven and all the people of Hallows End understanding everything that's happened." Breena swallows hard. "It's my intention and hope that while they'll need some gentle guidance, they shouldn't be pushed into chaos if it works the way I wove it."

"I'm confident it will work the way you intended, Breena, but let's lift the curse, and then we can worry about how to help all the people of Hallows End," Lucy suggests.

"Where do we start?" My mother looks nervously at the bridge and shuffles her feet. "I can't see the town. How do we get there?"

"Wait, I have a question." Lorelei turns to Jonas. "Can *you* see Hallows End right now? Like, when you look over the bridge, can you see it? Or is it invisible to you until you cross the bridge?"

Jonas turns to gaze in the direction of his village. "I see it. I see the buildings and the lights from the glow of lanterns in people's windows. I can see it."

"Fascinating," Astrid says, shaking her head and wrapping her cloak around herself more tightly. "Let's free these poor people, Xander. How do we go about this?"

"It's going to be a Labyrinth spell," I begin and nod

to Giles, who walks over to the truck we brought and lowers the tailgate. In the bed of the pickup are many crystals and geodes, all in different sizes. "We need to place the crystals in a spiral, making a path. As we walk the path in single file, we'll chant the spell that will open a portal to Hallows End for us."

"And in the center," Breena continues as Giles carries the tapestry to her, "will be the tapestry. We've mounted it to this stake, and we will draw some energy from this, as well."

"It's beautiful," my grandmother says, stepping forward to get a closer look. The beads and shells glimmer in the firelight, and Grandma traces her finger over the people celebrating their liberation around the fire. "Breena, this stitchwork is absolutely wonderful. But more than that, it's powerful. I can feel the magic pulsating off it. You are an incredibly gifted witch, my dear."

"Thank you." Breena kisses my grandmother's cheek. Is she thinking that she's related to my grandmother thanks to the reincarnation? Perhaps.

This is going to work, I hear Lorelei say in my head.

Yes. It is.

We all get to work as a team, hauling crystals over to the small clearing by the bridge and placing them carefully until they form a path wide enough for one person at a time to walk it in a large spiral.

Giles brought us tourmaline, obsidian, smoky quartz, and tiger's eye. There's also amethyst, rose quartz, and carnelian. Crystals with powers of protection, productivity, calm, love, and everything in between are represented on our path to freeing the people of Hallows End.

As we place each stone, I feel the energy building within me and in the air surrounding all of us. The anticipation and adrenaline coming from every witch here is palpable. It's so late, past midnight now, and everyone should be exhausted, but they're not.

Young and old, we're all revved, ready to finish a task we've been working on for over a year.

The excitement alone has a heartbeat.

Jonas and Breena erect the tapestry in the center of the spiral at the end of our path, the image facing the bridge. They hug and say something the rest of us can't hear and then walk back over to join us.

"This is just gorgeous," Hilda whispers next to me, shaking her head as she takes in the whole scene. "And maybe the most important thing I'll ever be involved in as a witch in my lifetime. It's overwhelming in a wonderful way."

"It's humbling," someone else agrees.

"I can't tell you how grateful I am to have each and every one of you," Jonas says. "Thank you for using your magic to help me and the people I've loved for centuries."

"You don't have to thank us," Lorelei assures him. "We're your family, too. Your coven will be welcome to join and become a part of us—if they want. We love you."

"I, especially, love you," Lucy chimes in and kisses Jonas's cheek.

"This shouldn't be difficult, but there will be many working parts. For the sake of simplicity, I'd like to explain things step by step. Mostly so I don't confuse myself in the process."

Everyone chuckles with me, and I continue.

"When you reach the center of the spiral, I want you to come together as one. Hug each other and continue to chant the spell as the energy builds. If you're claustrophobic, you might want to be one of the last to go in so you're toward the outside."

Several people grin, and I begin speaking the spell while they all listen, ready to follow my lead.

"I call on the wind, water, fire, and earth to follow us down this path of rebirth. Gods and ancestors, guide us we plead, show us the way to free those we seek."

As they learn the spell, their voices join mine, and the first of the coven begins their walk down the spiral path as they speak loudly.

The wind kicks up around us, gently at first and then with more energy as our voices grow. The six of us hang back and form a circle on the outside of the outer rim of the spiral, lifting our arms and beginning the words once more, with more force and strength this time.

The tapestry begins glowing as witches reach it, hug it, and then each other, coming together in power and love, in perfect trust, lifting each other up. The beads and shells in the fabric glimmer in the glowing light.

I physically feel my third eye open as color surrounds us. Bright blues and purples start as our crown and third eye chakras open, then down farther through our heart and solar plexus, surrounding us in green and yellow. Finally, our sacral and root chakras open with orange and red, joining the other colors around us. Suddenly, it's a symphony of color, as if we're inside the aurora borealis.

"It's opening," Lucy calls out, her familiar, Nera, dancing at her side.

With one look at the bridge, I can see the portal opening like something out of a science fiction movie, with sparks moving in a clockwise direction and a bright, glowing yellow light in the middle.

"Let's go," I call out. "We'll keep the portal open. Don't be afraid."

Without hesitation, everyone moves to the bridge and over to the edge of Hallows End. They don't question whether or not we might become trapped there. They simply trust. That, in and of itself, is possibly the most humbling experience of my life.

"No freaking way," Giles breathes, his hands on his hips. "I mean, I *knew* it was real, but—"

"I understand," Jonas replies and steps forward, then turns back to us. "Please stay a few steps behind me. You don't have to hide here but let me go ahead and enter first."

"The five of us are right behind you," I reply to the other man, who nods. I can see the reassurance on his face that we're all with him as I turn to the others. "The six of us will be in the lead, and I'd like for you all to stay close behind."

"We know what to do," Percy assures me. "Let's get going."

Jonas's steps are sure and quick as we make our way into the small village. I hear gasps and chatter rise behind me, and I understand the nervous energy coming from the coven. The fact that this village, and all the people who live here, have been mere yards away from Salem for more than three hundred years is unbelievable.

And yet, here it is.

"I'm going to run to each of the homes and ask them to come out to us," Jonas says, already walking to the first house. "This is Louisa's house. I want to start here."

"Whatever you think is best," Lorelei assures him.

I narrow my eyes and watch as Jonas comes back out with a frown. He says nothing, just hurries to another home and then another and another before returning to us.

"No one is inside their houses," he says, shaking his head. "This is completely new. They should all be asleep."

"I hear noises coming from that building," Breena says, pointing down the dirt road.

"That's the tavern," Jonas replies, and we all begin walking that way. "There's no reason for everyone to be there."

"Let's check it out."

Something tells me to stick close to Jonas as he

approaches the door of the tavern. When he opens it, we see at least fifty people inside, all standing together but not speaking.

Not moving.

Protect yourself, I immediately say to Lorelei, and I can hear her telling the others behind me.

"What is the meaning of this?" Jonas demands.

As a collective, all of them turn in unison to look at us.

And all of them have black eyes.

"Out," I command Jonas and immediately begin a spell to trap all of them inside the tavern.

Jonas joins me, adding his magic to mine.

"Erect a wall, this ward we place. Keep darkness in this central space. Let nothing out 'til we say okay, our powers are greater than evil this day."

"What in the hell is happening?" Giles demands as Jonas and I return to the others. "I saw them. Their eyes—"

"I wasn't anticipating this," I interrupt and drag my hand down my face. "But *it* is here."

"How?" Breena demands. "How can that be? And what in the hell are we supposed to do now? We need the people you and Jonas just trapped in that building."

"I warded them inside a barrier spell so they're *safe*," I reply, my mind whirling.

"We can do this," Lorelei says, her voice perfectly calm as she reaches out for me and gently touches my arm. "*We* can do this, Xander. They're safe in there. Is it the whole coven, Jonas?"

"Yes. I don't know how *it* trapped them and got them in there, but it looks like it's everyone."

"Then they're safe," Lucy agrees. "And Lorelei's right. We have the spell; we have the tools. We will lift this curse tonight."

Taking a deep breath, I nod and look back at my coven. Most of them are smiling. Nodding.

They're ready.

"Where do we go?" I ask Breena.

She closes her eyes and then turns to Jonas. "Where is the circle you stood around to cast the curse in the first place? With the fire?"

"Here."

Jonas motions for us to follow him, and we hurry behind him. We reach a large fire pit rimmed with boulders the size of small dogs. He flicks his wrist, and the flames leap to life.

"This is it," Breena breathes, her eyes big and full of wonder. "This is the scene from the tapestry."

I take a moment to look around and see that she's right.

"Did someone bring the tapestry with them?" I ask as I notice it's already staked in the ground right near the fire.

"It came itself," Percy says, catching my attention.

"What do you mean?"

"It has its own energy now," my grandmother adds

with a nod. "Can't you feel it? That's a powerful work of art."

"This is wild," Giles says with a grin. But then he looks over my shoulder, and his smile falls. "I hate to be the one who constantly asks questions like this, but who the fuck is that?"

CHAPTER TWENTY-ONE
LORELEI

We turn in the direction that Giles is pointing and see a man walking our way, striding quickly, wearing a simple brown cloak that almost hits his ankles. His hair is dark, and he has a beard.

But it's his eyes that have me on guard and widening my stance.

"Robert," Jonas says with a frown, stepping forward. "You weren't with the others in the tavern?"

"No," the man says, and then a smile spreads over his deceptively handsome face. Suddenly, I know without a doubt that *this* is the entity who's been fucking with us. The one who has been killing for centuries.

The one who murdered Agatha and tried to kill Breena. Who stood over me in my house and would have ended my life, too.

The one who possessed and tortured the love of my life just for the thrill of it.

"Oh, shit," Giles whispers.

"We haven't met," Xander says as he steps toward Robert, and I want to reach out and pull him back.

Be careful, I tell him silently. *You know exactly who this is.*

His only response is a slight nod.

"Robert," Jonas continues, "why are you not with your wife? Rebecca is in the tavern."

"Of course, she is. I put her there. I put them all there, and then you came along. You would dare to lock me out?"

He clicks his tongue on the roof of his mouth as he slowly paces back and forth on the other side of the fire from where our coven stands. Everyone is on guard. Even Nera, who hasn't left Lucy's side—and won't—is crouched, the hair on his back raised.

Even without looking around, I know that it's the same for the other animals who crossed with us.

"I never intended to reveal my identity to you," Robert continues. He's speaking pleasantly as if we're all the best of friends. "My intention was to kill those in the tavern and then come find all of you on Samhain, but now I have all of you here in Hallows End, and you've saved me the trouble. How convenient."

"You were under the curse, along with everyone else," Jonas says.

"I let you believe that." Robert smiles at Jonas. "You

really were a great leader, Jonas. You did everything right. Sure, you didn't plan on casting all your friends into a three-hundred-year purgatory, but you did the best you could with what you had. You know, maybe it's for the best that you know it's me. I have to tell you, it's been a *boring* three hundred years."

"You speak in modern English," I say, unable to keep the remark in.

"Sure. Just like Jonas here, I've been able to move back and forth. Well, part of me has. My body stayed here, but my consciousness can move."

"Did you kill a witch every year for their energy?" Xander asks, and Robert's eyes brighten, giving away the answer. "Of course, you did. That's how you were able to move back and forth."

"It's true. I have to come back here and replenish my energy between kills. It's quite annoying, really. But then you cast me out into the water, and I was able to get so much stronger there. As angry as I was in the moment when it happened, it turned out to be the best thing all around. Couple the water with all that delicious magical energy at that one's house"—he points at Breena—"and I was in the lap of luxury. You all made it so easy for me."

He pins me with his stare. "And you. Manipulating you with the music and turning the water against you was the highlight of my year."

"You're a sick fuck."

Robert smiles and rocks back on his heels.

"Why?" Jonas asks him.

"Because I'm a witch hunter, of course." Robert chuckles and rakes his gaze over all of us with a hunger I've never seen before. "I have gifts, and they get stronger when I kill those who have magic. So, I feed on you all."

"You're *married* to a witch," Jonas reminds him. "She carries your child."

"Brilliant, isn't it? What better way to ingratiate myself into an entire community than to marry into it? But I have to admit, *you* try being married to a pregnant woman for three hundred years. Holy shit, that got annoying."

I feel Xander shift next to me, and Robert narrows his eyes on him.

"I know that you're the strongest here, Xander, but you should be careful. I'm stronger here in Hallows End inside my body. I controlled you once before, and I can easily destroy you now. You're nothing more than a pest."

"Bullshit," Sandra says, stepping forward and not appearing frail at all despite being in her late eighties. "You're a bully, plain and simple. A spoiled, entitled bully, and we won't stand for that."

Robert snickers and then lifts a hand. Blue light shoots out of his palm at Sandra, but it stops just inches in front of her torso without hitting her.

Robert frowns, and then the expression on his face turns mutinous as Sandra laughs at him.

Sandra is one badass witch.

He raises his arms and pulls down lightning, and to my utter horror, he hits Lucy right in the chest.

"Lucy!" I yell. Jonas is already kneeling beside her. Nera cries and licks her face.

I can even see Agatha here with us, and she has Lucy's head in her lap.

"No, baby," Jonas says, cupping Lucy's cheek. "You won't leave me like this. Come on, Luciana."

Robert laughs maniacally. "Do you see how easy it would be for me to kill you all? With the flick of my finger, you'd be done. I've spent centuries getting stronger and learning. You can't beat me."

But Lucy's eyes flutter open, and Jonas immediately pulls her into his arms, hugging her close in relief.

Goddess bless our wards.

Robert sputters and then begins to rage, but then he suddenly stops, his eyes going round as he looks at something behind us.

I turn and feel my heart fill to bursting. All our spirit guides, all the witches Robert has killed over the centuries, and every one of our ancestors pour through the portal, ready to go to battle with us. To support us and feed us their energy and wisdom.

Sandra raises her hands as Lucy stands, her hand in her mother's. They begin calling upon the elements to aid in our quest.

"Powers of the north, element of Earth, we call on you to lend us your balance and wisdom. Powers of the east, element of Air, we call on you to lend us your breath, the very essence of life. Powers of the south, element of Fire, we call on you to lead us into action and control the chaos of the matter at hand. Powers of the west, element of Water, we call on you to connect us and help us feel."

Then they begin a spell I've never heard before. We're all listening intently, memorizing the words.

"Spirits of air, of land, and of sea, banish this evil and set us all free. No more killing, no freedom to maim, return this demon to the hell whence he came."

Simple but effective.

We raise our hands with her, making the same wide, commanding motions as we repeat the spell.

Robert builds himself a shield to hide behind like the coward he is, but it's not strong enough to protect him from all the magic coming at him for long. He launches himself into the air, and I can see that he's trying to draw energy from the atmosphere itself.

But he's not safe there.

Spirits rise with him, and with their hands linked around Robert, they bring him back to the earth.

Suddenly, he disappears altogether.

"Shit, it was better when we could see him," Giles yells as we all look around frantically, searching for the witch hunter.

"There!" Breena points to the tapestry. It's suddenly changed from a scene of celebrating townspeople of Hallows End and instead depicts one lone figure standing in the middle of the scene, his mouth open on a silent scream, and a look of pure fury on his stitched face.

Robert.

"Burn it!" Xander calls out as he and several other men rush to pull the stake out of the ground and toss it into the fire.

The heat and intensity as the tapestry ignites is insane. Suddenly, there's a sharp and loud scream, and the blackest smoke I've ever seen billows. When it clears, the very air itself feels different, and I know without a doubt that he's gone.

We've finally defeated him.

For a moment, we're all quiet as we simply stare at each other, taking it all in. The guides, ancestors, and dead witches all fade back but don't leave, almost as if they're waiting for something else.

"Now, how do we lift the curse?" Breena finally asks, her voice trembling. "The tapestry. Oh, goddess, the tapestry."

"That beautiful piece of art and magick did its job magnificently," Sandra says and then walks quickly to Breena, framing her face in her hands. "You may not have known it when you weaved it, but this is exactly what it was supposed to do."

"Lifting the curse is all about intention," I say, nodding as all the pieces begin to fit into place for me. "Yes, we have tools, but the power is within us. We have the spell words, and we have powerful magic full of the intention to free everyone in Hallows End, witch or not. That's how we lift it."

"Can we have one minute to do the bad-guy-is-dead happy dance?" Lucy asks, still holding her mom's hand. "Hi, Mom."

"Hi, darling girl."

"Goddess, I've missed you." Lucy hugs her mom close and wipes away a tear. "And I don't know what magic is letting me do this, but I'm so grateful."

"I am so proud of you," Agatha says. "And whether you can see me or not, I'm always here. Don't ever forget that."

"Maybe show yourself to me once in a while. Like, for my birthday or something."

Agatha brushes Lucy's hair off her face and kisses her cheek.

"I'm always nearby. Now, set Jonas and the others free, my powerful witch."

And with that, Agatha steps back with the other dead witches, ancestors, and guides. They all hover on the fringes of our circle, just beyond the firelight, but we know they're there.

"We're not quite done tonight," Xander says as he turns to address all of us. "We have the spell that was written to lift the curse, but we're going to need to use all our individual talents to complete it. We'll need assistance from all the elements again, as well as the planets, and we'll also need to use every trick we have up our sleeves. It's not a matter of simply reciting the words; it's putting every ounce of power we have into those words."

"We've come prepared," Shelly reminds him. "With all the tools at our disposal."

I turn and watch as several witches pull crystals out of their satchels and pockets. Others have wands or crystal balls. The cloaks they wear have magic embroidered into the fabric, with runes and sigils of protection and love.

I turn back to Xander and pull in a long, deep breath as I feel the energy around us begin to build once more, the way it did when we were out with the spiral during the Labyrinth spell.

"Breena," Xander says, turning to my cousin. "You begin the incantation so we can all hear and learn it. You're the one who knows it by heart. You wrote it."

Breena licks her lips and nods, moving forward.

"We all need to make a more connected circle around the fire, with Jonas at the head to the north, as it was when he first cast the curse."

We all follow her directions, evenly circling the fire. Some join hands. Others close their eyes.

Each witch will have to use the energy and wisdom that suits them for this very special spell.

"After I recite the words once," Breena continues, "we need to say it together three times. Then, we'll begin walking counterclockwise and repeat it another three times to banish the curse. Finally, we'll switch directions and walk clockwise, saying it three *more* times to bring in all our intentions. Each of you...as you speak the spell, visualize what it will look like when it's lifted. *Manifest* it into being. Think of how we will celebrate with the townspeople here and teach them what they need to know about the modern world. Visualize how they'll be our friends and part of our community."

"I love this," I murmur as I link my hand with Xander's. "What a beautiful way to lift the curse."

Jonas is incredibly emotional. He's not crying, but I can see all the hope and fear and love churning in his eyes. I can't imagine how much this must mean to him.

"Are you ready?" Breena asks. "Does anyone have any questions?"

"We're ready," someone calls out, and everyone else nods in agreement.

"Okay." Breena takes a long, deep breath, and we all instinctively follow suit.

And then, she begins to speak.

"Earth, Fire, Water, and Air, be the answer to our prayer. Banish this curse and leave these lands pure. Tonight we are the blessed cure."

We repeat the words three times, and then, as a coven, begin to walk very slowly counterclockwise.

I notice the wind first. Clouds form over the starry skies, and lightning streaks through them. Then, the rain begins to fall.

I raise my hands and use the power of the water to fuel me as we repeat the spell. I see others doing the same. Some, like Jonas, draw magic from the fire.

Lucy's feet glow, and I see she's pulling energy from the earth.

When we've finished moving counterclockwise and pause, I blink, automatically coming to attention when I see other people walking down the dirt road to join us.

"Jonas?"

"Louisa," he says in surprise. It looks like everyone from his coven was freed when Robert died and are now coming to join us.

I reach out with my mind to see if we need to protect ourselves from their fear, but they're not afraid.

They're curious and eager to help.

"Listen to the words and join us," I say with an encouraging smile. "Please."

Louisa, who is just lovely, returns the smile and nods.

"We will join you. And then I must know more about you. We know the words. We've been listening."

Jonas's coven joins ours, mingling into the circle, and once they're all in place, we begin the spell again, walking clockwise this time.

The energy is *unbelievable.* All the colors from earlier —the red, orange, yellow, green, and blue—are bright and vivid as we repeat the spell, mingling with the purple of our intuition and intention and haloed by the pure white of goodness and protection. The energy glows around us, pulsating, and if I'm not mistaken, I can hear the ancestors and spirits just outside the glow of the fire, saying the spell with us.

We're all working together, and it's the most powerful thing I've ever felt in my life.

After the last word has been spoken, Jonas raises his hands and says, "The curse of the blood moon is lifted. As we will it, so mote it be."

"SO MOTE IT BE!"

The fire shoots up into the sky as if in celebration, and then sparks fly, exploding into a grand display of fireworks.

"We did it!" I jump into Xander's arms as others dance and hug and cheer.

Jonas is hugging his friends, and when he finds Louisa, he kisses her forehead tenderly.

"Oh, my friend," Louisa says. "It is over."

"I have so much to tell you," Jonas replies, gesturing for Lucy to join him. "This is my wife."

Louisa's eyes widen in surprise, her hands flying to her cheeks. Then she laughs. "Yes, we have much to talk about, indeed."

"What is that light?" one of the townspeople asks, pointing toward Salem. "What are those buildings?"

Amazingly, the barrier is gone.

"That's Salem," Xander replies, moving to shake the man's hand. "And we have much to tell you."

"I can't believe we planned this wedding in a week." I'm standing in my bedroom, my mother fussing over my dress. "It's been so busy, what with casting the invisibility spell to put Hallows End in a sort of bubble to keep them safe for a while, moving Xander into this house, and all the other things. I don't know how we did it."

"We might have had some magical help." Mom winks at me as she fastens a clip to my hair with some shells and hag stones I collected glued onto it. "There, you're all ready."

I stand and look myself over in the mirror. My cousins and Hilda offered to help, as well. Hell, even Agatha is around here somewhere.

And Xander's mom and grandma stopped by earlier to see if they could do anything.

But I wanted this moment for just my mom and me. She finds my eyes in the mirror and rests her chin on my shoulder.

"You're the most beautiful bride I've ever seen."

"I think you said that to Breena and Lucy on their wedding days, too."

"And it was true on those days, as well." She smiles softly. "I'm proud of you, daughter. You're a strong woman who doesn't take any sass from anyone."

"I learned that from you."

"Damn right, you did." Mom smirks, but then she's serious again. "For a while, I thought you were lost to us.

I knew that you had to go out to California to heal whatever it was that hurt you so deeply, but I feared you wouldn't come home. As a mother, that was my worst nightmare."

"I'm so sorry, Mom." I turn and hug her tightly. "I'm sorry I lashed out and that I was so selfish."

"You had to be, and I understand. But I'm so happy you're home where you belong and that you're happier than I've ever seen you. Of course, I think Xander is a wonderful man because he *is* exactly that. But more than that, he's for you. You're both better when you're together. Trust in each other. No relationship is fifty-fifty. It's being there for each other when one of you only has twenty percent to give, and the other makes up the remaining eighty. It's give and take, darling. It's about choosing love, even when it's the hardest thing to do."

"You're right." I nod in agreement. "I didn't choose love when that's what we both needed more than anything. I'll remember that. Maybe I'll put a sign that says *CHOOSE LOVE* on my mirror so I see it every day."

"Not a bad idea." Mom winks at me. "Okay, let's get you out there to get married to that big hunk of a man."

"Mom!"

"What? I may be getting older, but I'm not blind, honey. That man is...wow."

I laugh and pick up my flowers, along with our handfasting cord, and take Mom's hand in mine as we walk outside.

The decorations are all beautiful, and perfect for

Samhain with fall colored flowers, pumpkins and the colors of autumn on the trees around the cottage.

Those we love the most are seated in chairs on the sand. Giles and Jonas stand next to Xander, and Breena and Lucy are already at the front, waiting for me.

And everyone is smiling.

A member of our coven plays the violin beautifully as Mom escorts me to Xander, who watches me with those beautiful black eyes of his. He's so handsome in his suit, so tall and broad and fierce.

But I know he's also gentle and kind and so in love with me that he gets stupid about it. I love every facet of this man. Every flaw. Every sexy inch of him.

He takes my hand in his, and I know without a doubt that I'm home.

EPILOGUE
AGATHA FINCH

One Year Later

I'm a grandmother.

My beautiful girl had a daughter this morning with her handsome husband by her side. Of course, I've already rocked that child in my arms as she got ready to make her grand entrance into the world.

Lucy will be a wonderful mother.

I just wish I could be with her to guide and help her. But I know that my sisters and Lucy's cousins will do for her what I am no longer able to do.

"Oh, look at this baby," Breena coos as she holds little Katie in her arms. Lucy and Jonas named their daughter Katrina Agatha, and I think that's an absolutely beautiful name. "You're so beautiful. Yes, you are."

"Let me see," Lorelei says as she nudges closer, smiling down at the pink face. "Oh, you're cute. Of course, your parents are cute, so that makes sense."

Lucy insisted on a home birth, as long as it was safe to do so, and my sisters were with her, coaching her every step of the way. Even Jonas's good friend, Louisa, came from Hallows End to help since she has training as a midwife.

Of course, that training is three hundred years old, but some things don't change too much, even with the passage of centuries.

Hilda looks over to where I'm standing and smiles. She and Astrid can always see me. It's a pact we made when we were children: That no matter which of us died first, we'd always still see each other.

I've held up my end of that bargain.

I know it'll be many years before my sisters join me here on the other side, and that makes me happy. I want them to enjoy their children and our grandchildren, and live to be very old women. I'll be here with them through it all.

But...oh, how I miss them all.

Sometimes, I wonder if it's a blessing or a curse that I can hover just on the outside, seeing their triumphs and struggles and even help them here and there. But it's not the same as being in the mix of it all or hugging and holding them. Laughing and arguing with them.

I miss it. Especially now that our dear friends Shelly and Sandra have moved back to Salem, completing our friend circle once more. I would love to sit at our table, sip tea, and conjure up all kinds of spells with my favorite women.

Deciding this should be one of those moments when my girl can see me, I step forward and watch as Lucy's eyes find mine. She smiles.

"You're here."

"Of course, I am. This is my first grandchild." I reach out and drag my finger down Katie's smooth cheek. "She's perfect in every way. And she will bless your life for many, many years. She will be a powerful witch, having inherited both of her parents' gifts."

"How do you know?" Lorelei asks me.

"She told me." I smile at them all and then look back down at little Katie. "We're already good friends."

It's been a wonderful year for my family. This may be the first baby, but it certainly won't be the last. Breena doesn't know it yet, but she has a little one already sleeping peacefully in her womb, and even Lorelei will have a surprise soon.

I always told that girl to never say never.

Watching how my coven has come together to help all the townspeople of Hallows End this year has been wonderful. They're giving history lessons, teaching them about money, and showing them how to live in modern-day society. There have been births there, too, and some deaths.

Ones that should have happened long ago.

Finally, after centuries, everything is as it should be.

There's no more danger. No more curse, and when the townspeople of Hallows End are ready, they'll merge into Salem to live out the rest of their lives.

What started with two little girls crying wolf in 1692 has finally come to an end.

"Can you hold her?" Lucy asks, nodding to the baby.

"No, but I can hold you." I scoot onto the side of the bed and pull my baby into my arms. It always diminishes my energy a little to touch her like this, but there are moments when we both need it.

Breena passes the baby back to Lucy, and we all sit, all of us women linked together. My sisters stand nearby, and Breena and Lorelei are at the end of the bed. We are the daughters of daughters.

"I love you," I whisper into Lucy's hair and look around at the rest of my family. "Oh, how I love you all."

NEWSLETTER SIGN UP

I hope you enjoyed reading this story as much as I enjoyed writing it! For upcoming book news, be sure to join my newsletter! I promise I will only send you news-filled mail, and none of the spam. You can sign up here:

https://mailchi.mp/kristenproby.com/newsletter-sign-up

ALSO BY KRISTEN PROBY:

Other Books by Kristen Proby

The With Me In Seattle Series

Come Away With Me - Luke & Natalie
Under The Mistletoe With Me - Isaac & Stacy
Fight With Me - Nate & Jules
Play With Me - Will & Meg
Rock With Me - Leo & Sam
Safe With Me - Caleb & Brynna
Tied With Me - Matt & Nic
Breathe With Me - Mark & Meredith
Forever With Me - Dominic & Alecia
Stay With Me - Wyatt & Amelia
Indulge With Me
Love With Me - Jace & Joy
Dance With Me Levi & Starla

You Belong With Me - Archer & Elena
Dream With Me - Kane & Anastasia
Imagine With Me - Shawn & Lexi
Escape With Me - Keegan & Isabella
Flirt With Me - Hunter & Maeve
Take a Chance With Me - Cameron & Maggie

Check out the full series here: https://www.
kristenprobyauthor.com/with-me-in-seattle

Single in Seattle Series
The Secret - Vaughn & Olivia
The Scandal - Gray & Stella
The Score - Ike & Sophie

Check out the full series here: https://www.
kristenprobyauthor.com/single-in-seattle

Huckleberry Bay Series

Lighthouse Way
Fernhill Lane
Chapel Bend

The Big Sky Universe

Love Under the Big Sky
Loving Cara
Seducing Lauren

Falling for Jillian
Saving Grace

The Big Sky
Charming Hannah
Kissing Jenna
Waiting for Willa
Soaring With Fallon

Big Sky Royal
Enchanting Sebastian
Enticing Liam
Taunting Callum

Heroes of Big Sky
Honor
Courage
Shelter

Check out the full Big Sky universe here:
https://www.kristenprobyauthor.com/under-the-big-sky

Bayou Magic

Shadows
Spells
Serendipity

Check out the full series here: https://www.
kristenprobyauthor.com/bayou-magic

The Curse of the Blood Moon Series

Hallows End
Cauldrons Call
Salems Song

The Romancing Manhattan Series

All the Way
All it Takes
After All

Check out the full series here: https://www.
kristenprobyauthor.com/romancing-manhattan

The Boudreaux Series

Easy Love
Easy Charm
Easy Melody
Easy Kisses
Easy Magic
Easy Fortune
Easy Nights

Check out the full series here: https://www.

kristenprobyauthor.com/boudreaux

The Fusion Series

Listen to Me
Close to You
Blush for Me
The Beauty of Us
Savor You

Check out the full series here: https://www.
kristenprobyauthor.com/fusion

From 1001 Dark Nights

Easy With You
Easy For Keeps
No Reservations
Tempting Brooke
Wonder With Me
Shine With Me
Change With Me
The Scramble
Cherry Lane

Kristen Proby's Crossover Collection

Soaring with Fallon, A Big Sky Novel

Wicked Force: A Wicked Horse Vegas/Big Sky Novella
By Sawyer Bennett

All Stars Fall: A Seaside Pictures/Big Sky Novella
By Rachel Van Dyken

Hold On: A Play On/Big Sky Novella
By Samantha Young

Worth Fighting For: A Warrior Fight Club/Big Sky
Novella
By Laura Kaye

Crazy Imperfect Love: A Dirty Dicks/Big Sky Novella
By K.L. Grayson

Nothing Without You: A Forever Yours/Big Sky Novella
By Monica Murphy

Check out the entire Crossover Collection here:
https://www.kristenprobyauthor.com/kristen-proby-crossover-collection

ABOUT THE AUTHOR

Kristen Proby has published more than sixty titles, many of which have hit the USA Today, New York Times and Wall Street Journal Bestsellers lists.

Kristen and her husband, John, make their home in her hometown of Whitefish, Montana with their two cats and dog.

facebook.com/booksbykristenproby

instagram.com/kristenproby

bookbub.com/profile/kristen-proby

goodreads.com/kristenproby

Printed in the USA
CPSIA information can be obtained
at www.ICGtesting.com
LVHW091056120923
757858LV00002B/5

9 781633 501676